The Hour After
Happy Hour

The Hour After Happy Hour

– Stories –

Mary O'Donoghue

The Stinging Fly

The Stinging Fly Press
PO Box 6016
Dublin 1
stingingfly.org

The Hour After Happy Hour is first published in July 2023.

2 4 6 8 9 7 5 3 1

ISBN 978-1-906539-99-3

Set in Palatino.

Printed in Ireland by Walsh Colour Print, County Kerry.

Earler versions of some of these stories were originally published in *The Kenyon Review, The Irish Times, The Common, The Dublin Review, SUBTROPICS* and *The Stinging Fly*.

The epigraph comes from *Collected Poems: 1920–1954* by Eugenio Montale translated by Jonathan Galassi and published by Farrar, Straus and Giroux, 1998.

The Stinging Fly Press gratefully acknowledges the financial support of The Arts Council / An Chomhairle Ealaíon.

For James and Niamh

Contents

Tu non ricordi la casa dei doganieri
sul rialzo a strapiombo sulla scogliera:
desolata t'attende dalla sera
in cui v'entrò lo sciame dei tuoi pensieri
e vi sostò irrequieto.

'La casa dei doganieri' by Eugenio Montale

You won't recall the house of the customs men
on the bluff that overhangs the reef:
it's been waiting, empty, since the evening
your thoughts swarmed in
and hung there, nervously.

'The House of the Customs Men'
Translated from the Italian by Jonathan Galassi

The Rakes of Mallow

We're not unhandsome. We're no George Clooneys either. We have frig all in the way of chin glamour. We have substantial eyebrows. We've sported beards at different intervals. We've gone the route of long hair. We've gotten blade one and rued the revelations. We shave and use balm. We leave a little hair over the ears. We've worn stonewashed when it was de rigueur and piles of GAP we got in the States. We cross the border to buy cargo pants and get our teeth filled. We still get called my little beaus by Sheelagh the newsagent. We know she hasn't had one in years. We set her giggling as is our forte. We leave with something to smoke. We know we'll smoke until a shadow on one of our screens says stop. We go to bars. We infiltrate discos. We walk home late. We horse into breakfasts at high noon. We're familiar with bad cholesterol and we're surprised there's a good one. We compromise our immune systems. We cry like infants over soccer. We expect bellies to obstruct a clear view of our shoes. We wait for the light to decline. We're a lot about easement these days.

*

We had no sisters. We lamented our thickness concerning women. We fixed to ask our mother. We bottled out when *What's Happening to Me?* was left on top of the VCR. We knew she hadn't much more to offer. We studied the college girls next door like ornithologists. We learned their seasons. We followed them spring to winter. We watched them from the dark copse at the bottom of our lawn. We noted eye-catcher dresses and high cork-soled shoes. We were disheartened by the change to drab browns. We lamented army surplus boots and the feeling they'd given up on round calves and the scoop neck. We let them smile at us winsomely and say we were good boys. We let them go off wherever college girls went off to after college.

We had no father. We heard him threaten to leave so many times that in the end he had to. We told people he went to war. We never agreed on the war. We went from Belfast to Gulf One to Bosnia. We told the stories at teenage birthday parties. We told them at weddings all through our twenties. We rained bricks and mortar on him. We sent shrapnel into his legs. We brought it to the surface of his backside some years after it had gotten buried. We witnessed him nearly rape a woman. We pulled him off. We conferred him with the medal of shame and draped him with the ribbon of dishonour. We stopped when our mother told us we were the shame. We rented him a bedsit in some grotty corner of London. We furnished it with broken bits and *Reader's Digests*. We saw him onto planes to America and Australia. We let him make a fool of himself with one woman after

4

another. We sent him to an early grave. We had him down for methylated spirits.

We met girls our own go. We scaled the convent school wall and fell face-first onto meadow grass. We trampled the nuns' cabbage garden and peered in windows. We took the wrong bus home because they said it had good-lookers in high quotient. We got dropped off outside a post office. We walked half the nine miles home. We stole thick memo books from the girls on our own bus. We paged past perfume models and ideal homes. We tore out favourite this and top ten that. We were determined to find ourselves. We ran across numerous references to a Tommy. We narrowed him down to a tawny illogically handsome lad from the other school. We read aloud the dreams of girls who called him a screw and a ride. We murmured their testimonies swearing he'd smiled at them or maybe even knew their names. We felt bad for them because we were romantics. We wanted to be Tommys but then again we didn't. We had an eerie conviction that the world would be a cold dawn to the likes of Tommy.

We went away. We went to colleges and transferred and nearly didn't finish and did with honours. We learned about serious drinking. We drank county council coffers. We waited on steps and in offices for grants to come through. We drank Scrumpy and Buckie and Lambrusco Rosso when the grants ran dry. We scrounged. We stole from our mother. We got the guilts and bought her a second-hand winter coat with a fake Astrakhan collar. We had sex for the first time during freshers' week. We didn't have sex until the middle of second year. We stopped and started and went biblical lengths of drought and had concurrent girlfriends. We caught shingles and scratched ourselves to steak tartare. We caught crab lice. We doused our crotches in Prioderm. We ran around screaming from cold chemical flames. We worked in burger huts and medical device companies. We signed up for The Sleep Lab and a clinical trial in depression. We earned half nothing.

We came back. We waited for jobs to land in our laps. We slept in bedrooms that smelled of doors sealed for four years. We learned more about serious drinking. We did hard graft in bars we used to disparage. We darkened the doors of old-timey taverns and we got a rep for standing our round when there were four or fewer punters. We admired the melancholy good looks of our fellow journeymen. We saw newness in every stale thing. We called Thursday afternoons our think-tank. We listed options and worst-case scenarios. We moved Stay Here back and forth between columns. We tried to find girlfriends while we distilled our options.

We took part-time jobs in builders' suppliers and sub-teaching science. We pondered the high-rising hems of teenagers' skirts. We made expeditions into Cork City to see what its women were like. We loitered round Erasmus visitants from Lisbon and Madrid. We seemed to be getting someplace with all of them. We expected the full-on every next weekend. We anticipated foreign savvy and finger skills. We got displayed on screens to mothers in Rome and Cologne. We were told to wave and say hola. We were laughed at. We brought premium blend coffee from Gloria Jean's back to our mother. We limited forays to our own streets only.

We packed in the town when everyone was rooting and sending out shoots. We watched them throng technology and financial services. We assured ourselves we were better species than the land sharks they would become. We thought about Melbourne but settled on New York. We touched the ground at JFK. We were met by a second cousin twice removed from reality. We rented a room in a house meanly fenced by wire. We lived by the rules of a landlady solid as ham and smelling of hydrangeas. We watched women in saucer-sized sunglasses and strappy tops that gave onto lots of other straps. We watched our second cousin flick his coffee stirrer like a riding crop. We found our own way when he ran out of painting jobs. We decamped from Yonkers to Red Hook. We stayed away from Cork people and Kerry people and any other emissaries of the nation. We flattered Upper East Side teachers and rangy midwesterners and got a fair distance with them. We learned that America was about getting run over and not knocked down. We learned that chocolate glazed and chocolate frosted were different things entirely. We got fat and ran it off. We got into fixing and flipping. We made money but never called it enough to go home. We exchanged it for euro and slid notes between secondhand book pages. We told our mother to look for what might've really happened at Chappaquiddick. We never admitted tight throats at her letters on small lined writing paper. We never let down our side. We watched the towers come down. We listened to fighter planes scissor the evening. We told our mother we were fine. We never admitted feeling dread.

We veered close to the margin. We never crossed the hard shoulder. We wondered if some vital trait was missing in us or in the women we nearly married. We made no improvements and no lamentations. We got on with it. We met women from Woodlawn to Park Slope. We learned the word abortifacient. We spent a summer scouring for Irish students at the bars. We got cooked spag-bol in tenement houses. We flagged in humidity and the baste of our own sweat. We acclimatised. We telephoned cousins to sympathise on the death of uncles. We got a reputation. We got nicknames. We put money away in credit unions. We upgraded to ten-year-old whiskey aged in oak casks. We fell in love at some juncture or other. We commiserated the endings. We thought we'd do well with kids. We took laptops off our laps for fear they'd lower the count. We did our best to embrace the present and live an awakened life.

We went home to hold our mother's hand. We informed her fifty times a day who we were. We told her not to be frightened. We took advantage of her muddle to ask about our father. We got told he was gone to work without his lunchbox. We learned he drank Mi-Wadi orange like it was the elixir of life. We put up with her giggles and sheet-plucking when she said she couldn't talk about his wanger. We buried her in earth so hard a gravedigger tore a ligament. We didn't cry at the ropes abseiling her to the bottom. We ordered a headstone shaped like a heart. We added a pensive angel at the last minute. We called her a dearly missed mother in the company of heaven. We called ourselves loving sons. We drank through the stocks of two bars. We put her things out for charity. We kept a pair of Clarks shoes she loved even though they were worn to a ravelling. We framed a photo of her in a hat at the Galway races.

We unfastened ourselves from New York. We shipped home what we wanted. We knew there was no such thing as a ship when they said shipping. We declined Priority. We made goodbyes to few and far between. We took our second cousin out for a slap-up. We toasted him as our first and best man on the ground. We foisted money on him for doctor's appointments. We looked for the women who'd made a mark. We didn't find them or they wouldn't entertain a last ride. We listed what we'd learned from them. We were pleased it wasn't restricted to cuisine or the best placement and use of tongues. We sold a house to a man who said he needed more basement than house. We kept a house for renting. We went to the doughnut place and the window filled with Christmas balls in June and the whispering gallery at Grand Central. We closed accounts.

We elbowed our way back in. We found the foreclosed and the half-erected and we bought them. We got tarred as scavengers and buzzards. We got wanted by women we didn't want. We earned the last pints in the barrel and the small corner table at the house of pizza. We razed and rebuilt our mother's house. We sold it to a doctor and her doctor wife. We revisited religion. We gave money for new windows at the community centre. We went to all the matches. We worked our way back in. We said yes to women with teenage children. We got called fly-by-nights less often. We sailed in with ideas for a yoga hotel and a racecourse and a casino. We got laughed at and told to stick to gussying up houses. We chose red meat and chianti. We asked out Sheelagh the newsagent. We got scoffed onto the street. We know we'll try again another time. We walk the town and its hinterlands on sun-spackled evenings. We allow every day its own flair. We sleep in the fingerprints of our old bedrooms. We never have dreams in which we star for good or bad.

The Sweet Forbearance in the Streets

There's a good chance if she's nervous she'll tell This Thursday about the place called Mount Buggery, for she tends to burst out with things like that, things like its being next to a peak called Speculation, and how she found them on a list back in the months when she ate all of Australia from the internet. This Thursday wrote of himself that he loved to travel when he had the wherewithal, and she was impressed by wherewithal, something she'd put in the bucket of notwithstanding and irrespective, words you needed to run up to with a pole over your shoulder. Like Sergei Bubka, the first and only man to vault over twenty feet. She loved him twenty years ago when he said even after clearing twenty feet he had done some things wrong, his run, his hands, even the jump itself, which she had thought of as a lovely pleat of body over bar. She loved Bubka for being so tough on himself.

She'd love to know if This Thursday has pals who egg him on, tell him he's entitled to a good woman, to perfection even, that he shouldn't settle until he gets what his voluptuous appetite wants. She knows her own tuttlers want the best for her too, with their approving talk of mid-length haircuts and dermal fillers, how she was finally doing herself more favours now she'd let go of Big Ber. They had despised him for keeping her a living widow, and they brought her to a sea-town hotel, dinner, drinks, a big bedroom with two double beds where they all crash-landed in baubles and finery at three in the morning, two days after the funeral eight years ago. Big Ber is dead, they said at dinner, and she said, Long live Big Ber, and they swore in the struggle with the rubber cork on a Grüner Veltliner, told her she needed more, and would she ever cop on to herself. They were never more appalling as when they called the waiter over to tell him he was a fine young Italian stallion. He said he was from Poland, and they said they'd hardly believe him, with his swarthy looks, but it didn't matter, for a fine thing was a fine thing and things of that nature crossed all borders.

This Thursday is what she calls them, even though they have their own false names, because she'll only meet them that day of the week. The kind of day you do things like bank and fish counter and phone bill, but a day which nonetheless softly taps the accelerator to the weekend. There have been only three This Thursdays, over the throw of four months, and the girls are calling for less discrimination and more trawling the plentiful fish. They're saying even Jesus couldn't have made the abundance. All the haystacks, the lawkies, the chancers, the semi-solids. They're calling it the gift of choice. They say she can throw back the pike and tench. They're loving that she's doing it and not they. And they tell her Small Ber would be chuffed, entrepreneur that he is, mover and shaker, go-getter and all. Little grasper, she's tempted to tell them, grasping little nit.

Early on it was both sad and lovely, both lonesome and heartening, Small Ber gone to Australia, not sure how long for, not knowing if there'd be work, all of the unknowns that made it a thrill for the two of them. She told him it would be no shame to come home. She took pride in the first night she slept without the landing light. She sent him money by wire transfer. She Googlemapped his address and was vexed by the wide blowsy tree obscuring the door, the four-wheeled motorbikes with small stout tyres, the feeling that fifty people were living in there. Every blind in the place was down.

He worked in nearly the biggest shopping centre in the country, mobile phone promotions, glib speak and the sell-sell she heard when he tried to wind down calls with her. They Googlechatted when it was convenient on his end, which meant sitting in a blanket for an hour, more, watching satellites and stars sail across the Velux window until he pinged. Sometimes she drank a second glass of merlot, knowing full well it'd entail a metal clapper in her forehead the next morning, but it was worth it for the dark bouquet, the stiffening of the tails of her nerves.

She told Small Ber about the strange placenames she found, how that Australian novelist she liked was from a town called Bacchus Marsh, only she couldn't remember his name, and that was the fault of the placename and not the books, which she loved and recommended and gave as presents. Small Ber looked at something outside the screen, said those names were hardly any weirder than Ogonnelloe. She had the feeling of someone else there, several, an audience, hands over their mouths not to burst out. His hair was longer, rat-quilled on top. Highlighted it looked, frost tips they called it, or maybe just the sun in the kitchen in Doncaster. Blatant good weather, like her Touche Éclat Le Teint, making all things better and brighter. She asked him if he'd thought any more about coming for Christmas. He said by the time he got from Melbourne to Kuala to Dubai to Glasgow to Dublin to Clare he'd only have time for a turkey-and-stuffing sandwich before turning around again.

She told her first This Thursday about it, how it didn't gut her but made her proud, having a son that long of a haul away, a son doing well for himself, better than most, an assistant manager, with maybe promotion to regional manager down the line. A son taking in this amount, a son with that number of people working under him. This Thursday said she would be well-looked after down the line, then, a son that capable, an economy like Australia, and the respect, he emphasised, the respect for basic decent working people. He said he'd have gone himself, only he didn't have a chance among all the young bucks. He tried to sell her a heating system for her house she could zap on and off from her mobile phone, even if she was on the other side of the country. She pictured a plumb line going right across the country. Arklow. He lamented all the robberies lately, the copper piping stripped, water cylinders ripped out, the lack of respect for basic decent folk. He tried to sell her an alarm system she could zap on and off from her mobile phone. She finished her coffee and poppy seed cake and told him she had to go home, to barricade the doors, she thought to say, to stay inside and wait for them to come, as come they would, if his worldview had a say in the matter. She tongued poppy seeds from behind and between her teeth and left a euro under her cup for the cheery pregnant girl who served them.

The girls think Small Ber looks gorgeous with a bit of a tan. She thinks he looks like a bit of a pimp. The girls are wowed dead by the good looks of his girlfriend. She knows he's not coming home any time soon. Australia does that to them all, whether they go there from Ogonnelloe or Galway or Dalkey. It stops them being able to come home. They're always off on another trip, hours of driving, often days, just to reach some rock formation or waterfall others said they just had to see, not to leave Australia without experiencing it. She doesn't understand all the talk about experiencing things, flinging somewhere far, doing something daft, taking a photo. Never shutting up about it, like her cousin who was in Sun City when Frank Sinatra sang there, who clanged on about apartheid and boycott and how it was wrong that old-blue-eyes sang there, but how he'd never have seen him otherwise, so it was worth it as an experience.

Her second This Thursday assures her he gets it. She can tell he wants to get it, all the soppy detail he doles out, the only daughter who went to Canada and brought her two children with her, how she emails photos of them every few months. They panic him, he tells her, with their height and good looks and white teeth and radiant optimism. He wonders if they think of him much at all. He's dramatic and morose, This Thursday, looking out the restaurant window into the Ennis rain as if it held gentle answers, saying he's probably just an envelope containing money for their birthdays. He's forward, too, in spite of the melancholy, or maybe because of it, suggesting she'd be better off staying the night in town, saying the Auburn Lodge had a hot tub, reaching across the table as if to take her wrist but stopping at the sachets of sugar.

She'd tell the girls about This Thursday, and they'd be titillated, shrilling she should've gone for it, a roll, a frolic, a bed and a breakfast. What was there stopping her? Fifteen years ago they all watched the programme about Brit expats in Mall- and Maj- and Minorca, all shrank back at louty fifty-somethings at pools' edges talking about cocoa-oiling and Rolfing one another's hidden bits. They castigated the state of them, awful disgraces altogether, no shame, more money than sense. Now they were vetting for her, choosing from passport squares as glum as the KGB or a red-faced wedding snap with someone's attempt at The Rachel visible on his tux shoulder.

Small Ber tells her he needs a top-up, says it's so he can go to Alice Springs for a training and motivation course that'll help him climb the ladder faster. She looks up Alice Springs and doesn't think there can be much going on there, unless the course sends them into red rocks and blistering sand for endurance and breaking down. She tells him she's not flush at the minute, that the felt has to be replaced on the garage, and the fridge isn't defrosting properly. She tells him there's talk of flexi-time at the pharmacy, which everyone lip-reads as cutbacks. Truth to all of it, but she's firm in herself that she needs her moiety for refashioning, hair, jackets cut natty on the bias, travel.

Her latest This Thursday has run to three Thursdays, and she's nearly ready to take him up on the Christmas trip to London, the West End, the musical about Frankie Valli, a lovely Mayfair hotel. She tells Small Ber the camera isn't working on her laptop, so can they just talk instead? She tells him she hasn't the money to hand, but might she give him a portion of it instead, would that go towards, mightn't it cover the travel to Alice's Springs. Alice Springs, he growls, not Alice's. Not like the restaurant, then, she says, and he starts the ramp-down to goodbye.

She's fairly sure she won't make the trip to London, but the courting towards it, the coo-talk of restaurants and museums, the Victoria and Albert, the Tate, sweetens her enough to let it run awhile. This Thursday telephones every night after the news. She's sorry now she agreed to the phone calls. At the time it seemed the decent thing, the natural progression, and she does like his voice, the coffee-ad timbre, the throat-click announcing a change of gear. London, some French restaurant where lunch costs sixty-five pounds, but it's starred, and it comes with wine by the glass. He recaps on the headlines, and she lets on to mull them, humming and hawing agreement about tribunals and Merkel and cuts to the bone, even though she hasn't tuned into the nine o'clock since the start of austerity.

Bed will surely come into the picture if she goes to London with him, and she'd be ready if it did, ready, she'd like to think, in a sweet and pliant way. Ready like a cigarette, prepped to be flared or broken in half. He asks if she read his email with the hotel photos, and she did, but she won't mention his caps-locked note about THE BOWER ROOM, all tapestries and walnut, and the fact that he used the word *irregardless*, which even the best pole vaulter in the world would break his back on. He wrote that he would go to London irregardless of whether she did, but that nothing would please him more than to enjoy the city with her. The straight arrow disarmed her and made her queasy. She'd never tell the girls.

It's only that it's easier to think about going than going itself would be. It's kinder not to mention the senselessness of irregardless. If Small Ber were to stay in Doncaster, marry the leggy nurse, children, sprogs she thinks the Aussies call them, and decided they needed her near, she wouldn't. One of the girls' brothers cajoled their mother into decamping to America. She was back in Aughinish after a month and a half in Palo Alto. She couldn't, she testified, she just couldn't weather the sweet forbearance in the streets, everyone wanting everyone else to go ahead, you first, they insisted, please, you first.

Safety Advice for Staying Indoors

The farmer's daughter began her fifth period, more excavating, more mortal than the previous. The toilet under the stairs flushed half-heartedly, returning red-brown effluent. Go down, go away, be off to the underworld! She pumped a second time, jangled the handle to make her point. But there would be more. Dark clumps and entrails, another six days of the end of the world.

A schoolfriend had been on a winter holiday in New York and said the toilet at their aparthotel was space-age.

Legend! Like an egg, she said. And the lid lifted and closed by itself, and a night light under the lid. And Bluetooth.

A *what* toilet? The farmer. Her family wasn't that kind of family, he told her. They didn't have smart toilet money.

It was the trip she was keen on. The whole package, bagels as big as tractor tyres, Top of the Rock. Giant stone lions minding a library. Legend. The schoolfriend's NYC haircut got more artful the more it grew out. But the farmer's daughter didn't tell the farmer any of that. She'd be told they didn't have New York money.

This weekend nobody was going to New York. They had to stay indoors, no buts, ifs, or ands. Indoors was mandated by the news, the weather, the knife-faced government minister tasked with emergency. Even the youngest, blithest meteorologist had looked rattled. When every day of last year's heatwave boiled the mercury of the day before, she had smiled and bade everyone enjoy. But last night her voice was coldly instructional. She described an extreme wind field at sea, gathering force and making its way to the coast. Her map was swagged with white weather. She implored her viewers to abide by the precautions. The farmer's daughter wondered if the meteorologist lived for this once-in-a-lifetime call. From coast to coast, from point to point.

Her father went to the supermarket early in the morning.

I'd like you to put down a few things, he said. Things you like in case we can't go out for longer than they say.

He used squared paper and wrote in capitals. BUTTER MILK JAM HAM, and on it went, the useful, humdrum stuff of the fridge and cupboards. She added Cheetos and chocolate and ultra-thin pads that said teen on the packet. He slid down his glasses, read carefully.

Right, I'll see how it goes. Right.

He went through the door still reading the list, to the car, and rolled off into the world.

She read about a pill that suspended your period for many months. Side-effects included headache, breast pain, nausea, constipation, and diarrhoea. She would accept all these conditions in lieu of pain that rummaged wide and deep, and blood as dense as animal liver.

*

The farmer brought the weanlings to the shed and closed the door on the last of their skittish backsides, then put the groceries away. From the kitchen window he descried his adult animals in the second field north. Top corner, ranks tightened, they stood with their heads pooled together like politicians.

What did they know about endurance he didn't have a clue about? What secret skills had amassed in their marrowbone over generations? He couldn't remember the name of those ancient long-horned cattle with chests like winter cowls. They must have passed a thing or two down the line. His father and men like his father always called their farm animals *the beasts*. Their dogs, though, were creatures and pets and dotes and old loves.

He lowered himself into the chair in the bright front room where the sleeker, more modern things lived. It was a giving leather, a pale wood frame. He remembered all its slender limbs on the floor, his wife slotting them together. One Sunday she assembled two such chairs, along with other items she said would be more useful than he could imagine. Everything came flat-packed with doodled instructions. She promised to do it all.

He still found stray wooden dowels and plastic caps to camouflage screw heads. A set of blue shelves remained wrapped in plastic.

Harley moved under the chair on his belly, a low, ruthless hustle like a trainee in a terrorist camp. The beagle was smellier than usual from stress. He had arrived to them in a small crate the farmer knew was an old badger trap.

The farmer's wife had lofted the pup like pride and then dropped him on the table. He stank, her eyes watered. She said he reminded her of an ancient, rotting man who sat in front of her in church years ago. The dog was folded in shame under its absurdly long soft ears.

Still, she said, sometimes it is necessary to reteach a thing its loveliness.

She brought the dog to her shoulder, where it crooned with safety and desire.

Now it wouldn't be long before his daughter got vexed at the dog's rankness, shouted *Piss OFF* when he went to her door like a pedlar. There was never anywhere enough for him to go, except another room, and another, from which he got expelled in due course.

How had his wife come up with that thing about teaching and loveliness? She read a lot, committed things to memory. He had always admired the wise, sometimes cryptic stuff she dealt out like cards.

The farmer's daughter spent an hour searching for portents, toggling between almanacs and Nostradamus. In drawings the old seer looked highly fretful. His eyes were large and sad-rimmed. *Water shall be seen to rise as the ground is seen to fall underneath.*

This is a bad omen, her father had said on Saturday night. Bad, bad, bad.

He was texting her aunt back and forth about a meeting time for drinks.

She's telling me to wear something short-sleeved and nothing dour.

The farmer's daughter said that seemed like good advice. She liked watching her father behave like a pissed-off brother, hitting the keyboard hard, putting the phone down on its face and walking away.

She stood up from her screen and ounces of blood plummeted to the pad. In ancient Rome someone had the job of telling fortunes and futures from the guts of dead animals. Someone was probably doing this with period blood right now. Monetising with ads from pads and tampons. There was an influencer for everything.

Her father called Harley to his food in a gushy voice given to only the dog. Sometimes he sang to Harley when he thought he had the place to himself.

Hey there you with the sad face, come up to my place and live it up.

Hang down your head, Tom Dooley, hang down your head and cry.

She wondered if he got her Cheetos, or if something as epic as a raging tempest would clear the shelves of every rubbishy snack in town.

The farmer was bored by waiting. What about bread, one loaf for fresh and one to freeze? He knew the basic operations, how much of what went when, but he didn't have the hands for bringing it all together on the table. And that, his wife insisted, was the one true route to good dough.

He could ask his daughter, say bread was the right thing to do in a storm. She didn't seem convinced about the severity, though. And maybe it would veer off course, leapfrog the whole country to piss on the old enemy next door. He flicked on the radio. Someone was personally injured, she said, by the way the older generation didn't take her and her generation seriously.

He checked the drawers for candles and matches. His wife would have drawn everyone from their lairs, out to some centrally located commotion like playing Twister or a board game. Scrabble, which the farmer hated. Balderdash he came to like, the nonsense laws and the daft acronyms. His wife's specialty was bluffing full and likely film plots. Her face gleamed like a river with truth or invention.

The farmer still slept stormily without her. He bolted awake with locked knees or an arm killed by his own weight. But lately it hadn't been as appalling as those first encounters with the no-man's-land in the middle of the bed. Then he woke up falling at speed or drowning in the Bering Sea. He missed the hard work he did to survive those sinking, choking nights.

Harley had been inconsolable, but he too got better by the day. He didn't spin frantically at the sound of bicycle wheels on the gravel. He stopped throwing himself like an asylum patient against the back door. For this new fortitude the farmer let him sleep beneath the bed, even if the room was foetid by morning.

The farmer's wife was missed more unremarkably in summer than in the raw, dark months. She was a fluorescent pink ankle sock that kept turning up in the dryer, a carton of rice milk each of them waited for the other to throw out. Whether peptides eye cream or sea buckthorn shampoo, she moved steadily to the back shelf. Soon one of them would surely take the initiative and a big black bag.

*

Harley shumbled away from the farmer's daughter's door after some disconsolate scratching. It had been raining blindly for hours, stopping short like the snap of a clapperboard, then more rain.

If she had her way the farmer's daughter would never go out again. The town and shops and school would be as remote and unreachable as oil rigs. She would like the roof to get torn off her school. River water move in sheets across the tennis courts, rise above the ground floor windows.

Last year two girls walked into the river. One in winter, another just before school broke for the summer. Everyone went to the evening viewings. The funeral home had a low ceiling with pocked tiles. Beside a garage, it whiffed of engine oil and diesel. Doors were open to the street. A man walked by with a sweating bag of chicken, a drumstick raised to his mouth. He lowered it slowly, and fastidiously he folded it back in the bag. He bowed his head and moved on.

The bruise on the first girl was a painting. It was murmured she knocked against a stone outcrop under the bridge. Her face shrank back from that bruise because it was the most vivid thing in the room.

The second girl's hair was drawn back in stiff strokes. Powder clouded the baby hairs along her jaws and she wore a matte pink lipstick. It must've been the family wanted that face. It made her look older. Old enough to have known better, old enough not to have suffered.

Her own mother said there had been enough morbidity for one year. Or did she mean mortality? She looked up to the bookcase, as if the right word would come tumbling out like a leaf.

Whether or which, she said, it's tough enough a year for ten. They ought to fence off that fateful river.

The farmer's daughter went into and exed out of apps the school crowd used most. There were lines and affiliations. There was getting invited and being abruptly dropped. Her mother said it sounded worse than the Tudor court for flavour of the month and cruel disfavour. One app had a whispering option, and it bristled with conspiracies back in the time of the drownings. Lousy things were said about the father of the first girl and the mother of the second one. The father got words like perv and letch and interferer. The mother was given a sleeping pill habit and a boyfriend from the encampment by the motorway. The rough tribes, someone said.

The farmer's daughter watched the flames smoulder and get fanned to bright, new life. She wanted to say those things were lies or at least unlikely. But defending fathers and mothers, even the parents of dead girls, made you a laughing-stock. When she had said the History teacher was the only cool teacher they had, she was told go get her head examined. The History teacher was the first new teacher the school had in ages. The old one was called Bad Macca because he looked like a cranky Paul McCartney. The new one came to the town with a daughter. The daughter wore turquoise eyeliner and ankle boots covered in a dozen little straps. The teacher dressed in greys, garments like sailcloth that drowned a body.

The farmer's daughter watched the putty pot outside her window. It had been out on the sill for weeks, after her father glazed the windows. He said it was more satisfying work than he'd expected, and a big pay-off against draughts. The pot was full of rainwater now, meniscus shivering, fighting not to break the edge. She didn't blink until it spilled its lip.

At her mother's graveside her father's eyes had given up. They were banjaxed and savagely red, daring all condolers to gawk too long at his ruin.

Her eyes had held fast like a soldier's, but who would confirm this as fact? Her throat had filled with hot oil and her ears with a wheezing ache. Everyone, though, everyone corroborated the weather. How bright and mild and handsome, for March.

The wind was tacking harder now, groaning too. From under the chair the sound of high-speed licking, Harley at his phantom balls again. The dog delved and tended, comforting himself as best he knew. The farmer went round the windows, all with Xs taped on. The safety advice for staying indoors said take this precaution. It prevented glass bursting in hundreds and thousands when a window cracked under pressure. The farmer's daughter did them all with blue painter's tape, and the effect was neat and handsome.

The farmer should make her a cup of tea, rattle chocolate chip cookies onto a plate. Or a glass of milk and a bowl of Cheetos. They were a poisonous colour and a nasty extruded shape, but they were her choice and desire these days, so he got a few bags. Other than that, he was no good at getting through. She'd been rushing to her room after school. She'd been sliding from his view.

He ate a cookie in one bite to ease the sharp recall of Saturday night. But it rushed around him and wouldn't be thrown off. His own father once said when a woman was foolish, well, it could be quite becoming, but when a man was foolish, listen, that was just foolishness.

A few pints, his sister said. A bit of music! His sister was full of suggestions.

And his sister was first up for drinks. The bar was trying to stay abreast of the times. Craft beer and a garden, tiny lights on strings.

Lovely stuff, his sister said. But people looked sheepish in the twilight. The farmer was disoriented by talking and drinking outdoors.

His sister's friend said she adored the luminous skin of all the old folks.

It must be the damp air! Humectant. They look fabulous! She was American, and she hugged the farmer to meet him. She vowed the next drinks were hers.

She's a breath of fresh air, his sister said, isn't she, as the friend steered three ciders back to their bench.

The farmer saw other people watching him, watching them. The band wouldn't let go of Glenn Miller. The farmer asked his sister and the friend if they knew Glenn Miller had gone missing in an aeroplane. Flying to France to play for troops in the war, never to be recovered.

The friend thought that was Glen Campbell, no?

No, the farmer told her, Glen Campbell died only a few years ago. He said his mother and father had seen Glen Campbell sing 'Mull of Kintyre' in Dublin. An angel drenched in sweat, they'd said.

No way, his sister said! I never heard that! They never told me the same stuff as you.

He, a boy, had been repelled by their fealty to a country singer. Until he saw Glen for himself years later, in a shaky video, in a venue filled with heat and devotion, Glen picking up bagpipes and playing them like ready banter.

The farmer's sister went to play cards with an elderly couple looking for a third for Sergeant Major. She threw him a sharp, quizzing look. He kept talking, about Glen and Van Morrison and Luke Kelly. He summoned them all like friends for support.

Outside, the town had shifted on its axis. Bright-faced throngs, slim slow sliders. The farmer was tired and bleary under a new hotel's hot lit awning.

No to the nightcap, time to drop everyone home, the farmer was sure they understood, six miles in the other direction and all.

His sister insisted she get dropped off first. She looked away, swung her arm over the friend's shoulder.

In the farmer's car the friend mastered his face in a wide kiss. It was a searchlight panning cold sea for survivors.

My bad, she said.

Anyone could see he wasn't ready. She went in curt steps to her front door, the tall bright window. He waited until she found her keys. He'd hate his daughter to know about his long, silly minutes in the front seat. Not a word, he'd have to insist with his sister.

He turned the car sharp for the main road. His lights flushed out stone walls and trees. The gallant moment of bringing his wife home before she was his wife. Stoats on the verge, weasels' eyes in walls. She reminded him of the difference, the stoat being bigger, its tail dipped in dark paint.

Home to the large, dark house of her people, where there were never keys, where the door was always unlocked, where a huge light flicked on to interrogate his arrival in their yard. But still the farmer waited, until she got folded inside the wings of that old place.

He drained the nibs and dust at the end of the packet of cookies. He hadn't realised how much a person could eat when time was empty and for the killing. He filled a cereal bowl with Cheetos. They looked unexpectedly lovely in the white ceramic, like they were grown to glow as bright, healthy fruit.

The farmer's daughter named the last two Cheetos in the bowl Catherine and Heathcliff. She pressed them in a savage clinch and ground them to mush in her mouth. The kind of end they wouldn't mind. She hadn't decided if she liked that book or was merely hooked by it. It had the most melodramatic love-lines ever written, the kind that actors had to spit to say.

Yesterday she rolled a little paper to a grey pill. Plain words, an order. *Bathroom behind the gym, just after the last bell.* She set it on her tongue, moved it to higher ground behind a big back tooth.

The bathroom behind the gym had walls painted pus and trickling, squirting cisterns. A radiator banged like someone was fastened behind it.

Two weeks ago the first note from the History teacher's

daughter said, *I think I'm right about something. Something about you.*

The second, *When I did something dirty your face showed up in the mirror!*

The farmer's daughter should've been frightened, but something like this had been heading her direction. It was just a question of when and where.

The kiss in the back bathroom wasn't startling. It was clumsy business to be gotten past so the next time might be easier. The first time the farmer's daughter tried a tampon she duffed the whole thing. She'd done the calm-breath exercises, stood with a foot on the edge of the bath, inner and outer tube, the moves memorised.

None of it readied her for the insolent shock of settling matters to *a comfortable place where*, the leaflet said, *you ought not even feel it*. She pushed towards where she thought was the small of her back. Her hands jangled coldly when she pulled her jeans back on.

In the back bathroom, looking for somewhere to place or slot her hands, she remembered the word *footling*. The girl who got all the As in English class, an essay she read aloud about a favourite book not on the curriculum. *The Code of the Woosters.*

When the farmer's daughter's mouth footled and bludgeoned and skidded against the History teacher's daughter, it was a thing she might want again. Even if they got found out and slurred like filthy witches on the whispering app.

Anything else I can get you? Her father, a knock on the door. He said he was thinking of watching a film, only he didn't know what one, maybe she could choose.

You pick. I'll watch whatever.

She meant it and she didn't, but they could eat from trays like the days after the funeral. Lasagna from containers brought by neighbours and half-hour documentaries about agriculture or urban architecture.

Right, he said. I'll find something. I saw there was one about aliens and people trying to communicate with them.

Isn't that always the way, she said. Until they either eat you or leave you.

The electricity was butterflying, might go out before they got their film. The wind was relentless. Lids and barrels were rolling round the yard. A gate had come loose one field up, he knew from the exasperated sound of older metal, but he wouldn't chance going far in that tumult. Get hit hard enough not to get up.

He set the kettle going and looked for tea. The cans and jars cupboard sent shockwaves through the kitchen. Spiky bergamot and the hayfield swoon of chamomile. Stocked when his wife stopped drinking coffee. He pined for her coffee, that thing from her enigmatic life before him. She'd come with all its paraphernalia, small silver pots, smaller cups rimmed with gilt. Whole weekends infused with the scent of burnt rubber.

She'd always taken coffee, she said. In Dublin, then in Paris, then when she moved back to the countryside with her parents. She said they disliked the taste almost as much as he did.

When she moved to his house she had plans for design.

They sanded floors and painted walls and had sex more times than he was sure most people did in a day. And coffee, sour as smoke through the house.

Then tea boxes, coming by courier, the driver baffled at the small consignment in his hand. Ceylon Orange Pekoe. Formosa Oolong Spring Dragon. There were black teas and rusty teas, dried rose hips and organic gunpowder.

It was an education, she said, she was learning tremendous things about what went into tea. Fine grades and hand processing. Tender buds collected in highly controlled conditions. Sometimes one bud and two leaves. She would never wait for a kettle to reach full boiling, because that was too hot for most good, proper tea.

She used milk, even though it wasn't recommended for fine white teas and those made from berries. And she left half-finished tea round the house. The farmer found cups gone cold and cataracted. On the shelf of old DVDs above the television. Under the bed. He placed his mouth where hers would have rested. The old liquid trembled and issued a smell of turned earth.

It turned out the aliens film didn't start until later, by which time they'd probably be in darkness. There was something about an Irish emigrant girl in New York. There was a true-life murder case that the write-up said might or might not be solved. The farmer hated sinister, grisly stuff where women and children were victims and the voices of truth-tellers were altered for their safety.

His daughter sat on the couch just as he hit on the baking contest.

Yes, she said. Let's do this thing!

She drew cushions around her like a rampart. Her language had changed in the last year, become more derisive and elastic. Sometimes she sounded like one of the radio callers who got two minutes for railing and spleen. Or she was whimsically delighted by the smallest details. Pasta shaped like ears, a cruelty-free lip-balm. He rarely knew what she'd love or hate. He tried to keep up with the trends.

Right, he said! Let's do this thing.

She looked at him like he'd issued an insult.

The baking contest was tiresome. The camera ran around to see who was under pressure and who got their mirror glaze perfect. A plume of flour marked the spot where someone dropped a bag.

I love her. *Love* her! his daughter said of the older woman who visited stations and judged matters with increasingly menacing sweetness.

His daughter said if your sponge was dry, you were done for. The farmer counted waffle ingredients he knew to be in the cupboard. Maybe they'd make breakfast together in the morning. Do this thing.

The baking contest ended in someone crying because she didn't make the cut. Another contestant couldn't believe he'd gotten through. OhmyGod, ohmyGod, ohmyGod, he said through bright tears. The farmer's daughter could never compete for anything on television, not general knowledge or dating or cooking or sport.

Her father had gone to the sheds to check the animals.

Five minutes, five minutes, he said. I'm not going to end up dead.

She spotted the album from Portugal on the shelf under the coffee table. Her mother had taken good photos, insisted on printing.

Real people take out an album, she said, they *look* at it. They don't suffer the computer. Filenames and folders bedamned.

The hotel walls were exquisitely white and the pool a staring blue eye. There was her father, grinning lushly on a lounger, grinning again before diving in. There were precise photos from small towns and untrammelled beaches they drove to, lunches in restaurants where laughter surged from the kitchen each time the door swung open.

Most of the farmer's daughter's photos were crap. The elements never lined up because she was never fast enough to catch people at their best. Instead her mother's mouth was a livid line on the steps of a sixteenth-century church and her father's shoulder departed the arrangement. They were both dim and doubtful in a shop that shimmered with silk scarves.

She'd like to have filmed them from the balcony one evening. Her mother sang to her father, down by the pool. They were the last of the day's hedonists. Someone had built a ziggurat from plastic glasses. Boxed in light from the pool and patio windows, her parents were lean as whippets. They looked good in swimming gear.

Her mother's voice swam deeper in that melancholy song.

Love-o, love-o, love-o, love-o, love-o, love-o love, still falls the rain.

Her father came back from the sheds in a fluster. A Friesian was looking suspicious.

Like she's ready to calve. I know the look. Fuck. Like, could she have waited for worse conditions!

He cursed only in the extremes of farming trouble. Not politics, not cooking, not the sadness that sent him to bed early.

There's stuff flung all over the place. And I thought I tied down everything. Branches on the hens' house.

He was worried about a sheet of metal on the hay shed. It was loose and belting like a sail. He would wait until first thing in the morning, then straight to the Friesian with blankets and tarp.

Keep storage heaters away from flammable stuff. Wear shoes in case of broken glass. Have a battery radio. Don't depend on the internet. Listen for updates. Above all, listen for updates.

Her father clicked through channels.

Where, oh where, is that aliens film? I'm ready to settle down to something daft!

The farmer's daughter budged to get some comfort. It was time to change her pad. Hopefully the History teacher's daughter was following the protocols. She turned away from the farmer and kissed her forearm. Maybe she should send a note. She would be kind. In the note she would say they shouldn't meet like that again because they might get caught. She would say she needed to think about what happened. That probably they were practising for others. Nothing to be ashamed about. That was how the world worked. And the rest of the term would pass, she knew, in sad, baffled glances and high-effort evasion in the halls.

A branch raked its nails on the window by the bookcase. When Lockwood reached out the window at Wuthering Heights to grab a stormy branch, the branch grabbed him back.

Ten minutes until the film, so the farmer made tea from two bags. His daughter said she'd join him in a cup. He understood why people drank chamomile by night. It tasted like a snooze in a field in June. It didn't wire him to the moon like black tea did. Caffeine was the enemy of people with jumpy numbers.

He'd been given terrible blood pressure numbers at last year's visit. Systole, diastole, the very words were nasty, obstructing all attempts to spell them in his head. His doctor said it was bad luck.

How did we let it all go as far as this, the doctor marvelled?

Who were the *we*, the farmer wondered, in this equation. He tried to see round the doctor's shoulder.

But lucky they caught it now, the doctor assured him. He didn't like numbers like he was seeing here. He didn't like them one bit, but they were surprisingly common among rural men.

Welcome to middle age, the doctor said to the farmer. I play golf myself, to keep things in check. I suppose walking fields is the exercise you get?

Then the doctor said he had to ask if the farmer was stressed or depressed.

We have to engage a patient on that kind of thing, he said. More so the men. It's purely procedure.

The farmer said there wasn't anything bothering him, at least nothing he could think of right there.

The doctor was glad. He wrote a three-month prescription for the BP and told the farmer to look up a book on meditation.

The farmer could have told him that once or twice a week he was struck by a hot, throbbing pain that he loved his wife more than she did him. But it wasn't a problem per se. Merely a reminder of the common unfairness of the human heart.

The doctor added oatmeal and blueberries to the list of good stuff.

His daughter's chamomile was cooling off. She'd picked up the cup, put it down to go to the bathroom again. So much time in the bathroom, she might as well pay tax and insurance on that cramped, chemical place. He set the honey jar next to her cup, a spoon. Alien music struck up, sonar pings and the low boom of unexplored territory. The old television got louder for some things over others. His daughter shouted she was coming, and would he pop out the footrest? She loved the laziest seat in the house.

When his wife woke him in the dark heart of their last night, the room was impenetrably black and love a wordless panic. He sweated to make her happy. He worried awhile about his heart, the valves groaning like tight doors. In the morning her sleeping face was clear, serene, as if she'd been on a wonderful overnight junket up those tea mountains where they picked only buds.

They used the younger, prettier photo when she was a morsel of nine o'clock news. She was celestial in the top corner of the screen, smiling shyly above a crashed car.

The car lay on its back like an insect, no hope of righting itself. The driver had been drunk, a young man from another county. The farmer's wife had been on her evening walk, yellow fleece jacket, elbows going like pistons. The news moved on. An elderly bachelor's lottery win on the peninsula. The camera ogled stacks of turf behind the man's meagre home.

Later, after most of the worst was over and the rest hardened and contracted like mortar, the farmer's sister said she hadn't realised how like Meryl Streep his wife had always looked. Tremulous, watchful for those who would break what was dear.

He would watch a Meryl Streep film now, instead of the aliens. *Sophie's Choice* would be too heavy, though, *Falling in Love* too sad and antiquated. Better one where Meryl was older and funnier, flirty and easily sidetracked. Ruefully trying out love once again.

Then the wind went ninety and Harley bayed for pity. The air banged like a Lambeg drum. It was so startling it could have been a comical trick. He found himself wanting, sickening, in the panic. No know-how, no courage whatsoever. He shouted for his daughter to come down, come down now! And he wasn't able to decide among the photos of his wife. He slid two inside his shirt, one to each teat.

The farmer's daughter was in the bathroom when the lights went out. Rising from the toilet, she fumbled the workings of a fresh pad. She smacked it quick to her knickers, pulled up, felt the gum affix to skin and hair. Shitsticks. Her father was shouting. Time to get downstairs.

Rez-de-chaussée, she learned in French. Level with the street, perhaps to do with carriages and horses. Her mother always tried to get in on her homework.

Vous avez passé(e) un vacance avec votre famille. Décrivez le meilleur jour (200 mots environ).

Oh, oh, I'd need way, way more than two hundred words!

Her mother sought the writing prompts and the reading comprehension. She loved how French current affairs always seemed more serious, more engaged and intellectual, even if it was just a bus strike.

The farmer's daughter tore the pad free. Her eyes watered, her head rang with victory, like that one time she waxed above her mouth. She turned the cursed thing around. She felt blood in a warm spate on her hands. She aligned the pad as best she could and rinsed her hands against one another.

She patted the cool bathroom walls and found the door. The landing was wholly dark, an otherworldly realm that called for adaptation. A Russian artist painted a famous black square because he wanted to be the first to paint something that wasn't *of* something. No attribute of real life, he said.

She walked feelingly between the black walls, she moved inch-wise across the black landing. This might be what it felt like to be pregnant, one foot in front of the other in darkness, testing the ground for stability. The stairs met her with emptiness. The squeaky ones were silent when she tested their treads. The newel was dirtily smooth to her hand.

Her father met her in the hallway. Cumbersome as a wardrobe, smelling of sweat, he wasn't any way huggable, but still she did, clapping her hands to his thick back. In the worst circumstances, survivors always hugged in films. Sometimes they ground their foreheads together and thanked God for letting them behold one another again.

They moved to the utility room. It had one little crosshatched window and was toxically sweet from dryer sheets. Her father swept the flashlight to find whatever might be useful in a siege. He threw down a few beach towels for Harley, who took his spot with a lacklustre sigh.

He cast the light on her hands.

What's that on you?

Her blood, in drying stripes and hard dribbles.

Oh, he said. Oh, right.

She said sorry for the slasher film. She'd been blind in the bathroom. A mess.

Here, he said, extending the flashlight. I'd say you turned the back of my shirt to a cave painting.

He threw his arms wide, turned around ceremoniously. She held the light like a burning stick and moved it studiously across his back.

She couldn't believe he'd said what he said. His joke was an awful delight.

The scene wasn't Altamira, and it wasn't Lascaux. But when the resinous light got smoky and the blue of her father's cotton turned to limestone, a pot-bellied little horse appeared smeared on the wall of his shirt.

During the Russian Blizzard

The Ingushetian was a man with skills that flicked out like a Swiss knife. That was my aunt's valediction when he finished coving her guest bedroom ceiling and tiling the rinky-dink en suite. She wasn't sure if it was Ingushetian or Ingusheti, she said, and she'd hate to be as ignorant as her colleague who referred to Pakestinians and Iranis. Then he fixed a few other things, free gratis he insisted, shaky drawer handles and gutters throttled by leaves. He even lopped a bough or two. They were elbowing menacingly onto the back roof, and in a storm would crush the kitchen, he assured her. I'd seen that kitchen in photos. It was a furlong of chrome and white shutters.

She told him she couldn't let go of such a capable man. She researched and found the term to be Ingush. She offered to rent him that guest bedroom.

It was all above board, she told me, when I turned up in Boston that September, it was all entirely above board. I was at the kitchen island drinking her tea. My face was a blind oblong on the fridge door. After graduation I'd expected to get a big bite out of life, but nothing big wanted me.

Everyone I knew had hied to Australia. I did the books for a ten-seater terroir bistro in Dublin. Its potatoes came from Kildare and somewhere in Mayo there was a pig. It was always about to fold. I went out with the head chef, half-slept a night on the tussocks of his old futon, and decided to take the hoary year out. I bought up for Boston and my aunt's guarantee. Two months' fact- finding would get me a job. Besides, she said, there was nowhere better than New England in the fall. We drank from porcelain mugs and she made me take a second French pastry.

The Ingush man was somewhere in the long garden that fell down to the sea. My aunt was a radiographer who'd put her learning and time into work, developing and rising until her nose touched the surface and she was Chief Radiologic Technologist at a hospital where she'd screened, she estimated, some thousands of breasts. One Christmas, three Benedictines, and she told me and my sister big or small they all looked like sliced meat on the photo plate.

Carpaccio, she said quietly, then a second time, more slowly, surprised by and proud of the depiction. We looked down and folded our arms charily. She was my father's sister. She had bouts of imperiousness and grand generosity. Largesse arrived during lean college terms. There was repeated advice to never travel the world with boyfriends. We used to feel sure she'd rescue us into a brighter life someday. I suspected she looked in the mirror some days and turned away in disappointment.

His name was Ruslan and he was proud of it, he told me first thing, because it was the name of the best and most peace-keeping president of his country. He met me at the airport, ADELE FROM AER LINGUS held across his chest. Shaping up for forty, he was square of face and smooth-haired as a shampoo ad. He smelled of pleasant herbs like sage and lavender. You knew he would do things well and carefully. He cursed once in the snarled airport traffic. He said sorry. I said it was a thing of nothing. He laughed at that, a thing of nothing. I had a happy presentiment he'd start using it and keep using it until it came to annoy me.

We picked up speed on the road to the south shore. I'd been this way once before, two weeks in Cape Cod with a crowd from college, but I'd bypassed my aunt's locale. Now I was curious, impatient even, to see the road and the house and the rooms where she'd always seemed so content. Something rattled under the Honda's ribs. Ruslan said he was deliberately choosing to ignore it. I flicked through the CDs. AC/DC. Bruce Hornsby and the Range. Enya. In an effort to resurrect the banter lost somewhere along Pilgrim's Highway, I said AC/DC were due for a comeback. He said they'd never left, so they were not due for a comeback. He said I was probably too young to have followed their arc.

I asked him if Enya had been big in Ingushetia. He took the CD and looked at it a long while. He probably took the same serious slant to every topic. He probably measured everything with a set-square. His left hand on the wheel was steady and relaxed. Garbed in velvet and peeping like Bambi, Enya was now in his crosshairs. It made me wonder if he'd been a sniper at some stage. He had the look of militia, dark flak zipped under his chin.

I couldn't remember if Ingushetia was a warry hotspot.
I was suddenly disgusted by how little I knew or cared
about world politics. Ruslan would surely be conversant in
every Irish pitched battle and failed rising.

He left Enya aside and said he was glad, glad in the
cockles of his heart, that such an angel had never made
it to his country. He called it a toilet and a cauldron. He
pointed out new shingles loosened on a church cupola,
trees taken down here and there, all by last week's high
wind. He never stopped smiling, right the way to turning
up a steep driveway, a house on a hill, my aunt waving us
on with a straw hat.

In the first week I drank lots of flavours of tea, hibiscus,
Darjeeling, the green leaves my aunt steeped with a
virtuous grimace. I put in time on her slim silver laptop,
job searches, dating sites. My sister said I should post a
profile as soon as I fetched up in Boston. It's what people
did, she said, when they moved somewhere new. Hung
up their clothes, sorted their money, and gave themselves
a nickname, some outdoor pursuits, and the best smile
amongst all their photos. No convert like my zealous sister,
who met her fiancé across a speed-dating table in Ringsend.
I perused profiles. Grinning, tanned and hopeful, they
made me nostalgic for the scruffy Lebanese chef.

I replied to an ad for an entry-level accounts receivable
analyst. I got told I was too qualified. I answered an ad for
a bookkeeper. Growing firms wanted comptrollers! the ad
said. A Cambridge start-up called me for an interview. An
hour on the line ended in a vague tip-off about another
start-up that might be willing to orchestrate the visa they

said I'd need, but it was a long shot, because nobody wanted to pay for a visa in the tight economy.

I took a phone interview for a weekend job as a tutor for a college student. Accounting was his nemesis, he said, but he needed it to become an entrepreneur. He had big plans, he said, he saw opportunity everywhere. We agreed to start the following week, three hours on Saturdays, two on Sundays if they were needed for impending exams. His mother telephoned to cancel. She was concerned my Irish training wouldn't transfer. No hard feelings, she assured me.

None, I said. I postponed the job search and committed myself to self- improvement.

I researched Ingushetia. I studied its history of upheaval. It rose against Russia, against Communists, against Northern Ossetia, and lately there was trouble biting round the border with Chechnya. Suicide bombings, high-profile murders and kidnappings. Years ago they had a beautiful female sniper who had never been captured. Everything from its ancient three-handled pots to all the boxers and wrestlers it claimed as famous people made me sad not to have known Ingushetia sooner. An elderly woman at the small library sat with me. Together we ticked book after book for interlibrary loan. A lot of them had Ingushetia nested in studies of Russia and Chechnya. Many titles were in the Ingush language, parades of vowels umbrellaed by long accent marks.

I settled on an English book about counterinsurgency, disappeared persons, and human rights. The librarian said it would take ten days. She ran after me with another reference, a John le Carré spy thriller containing an Ingush renegade, and the library had it. I went home with the paperback. A man's silhouette stood in a door looking out on rocky escarpments. The sky was crimson melting to pink. It looked pulpy and compelling.

I fixed on the climate as a question for Ruslan. He reported it as summer beauty, sometimes brutal in winter. His father used to say, and he pardoned himself for relaying it, a person put their balls in a lunchbox in the freezer or they let January take them. I was sitting on the back deck watching a wasp disco round his arm. He was putting a new handrail on the steps and the deck. My aunt was in the rose bushes. Below the rose bushes the sea slurred and intimated. It was evening, the last Saturday in October. A dead blow hammer, Ruslan had told me proudly. Filled with lead shot, it struck hard and heavy but didn't mar the surface surrounding the nail. A beautiful idea, he said.

Earlier that morning he had assembled a new bed in his room. He was all for slats, he said, instead of the base they call boxspring, because slats kept a bed cool, and they looked cool in addition. His bedroom was at the back of the house. A mini-foyer, with a one-drawer desk and a mirror, separated it from the kitchen.

When Ruslan was finished, my aunt made the bed with new sheets, also cool. I helped her smooth corners and tuck under. I wanted to press my face into the waffle pattern. Then lunch was made around me at the island. Shrimp asleep on spinach leaves. Ruslan knew precisely when to fluff the cous-cous. My aunt suggested opening a bottle, just for the nice day that was in it. Ruslan took only half a glass. He had bookshelves to assemble. Allen wrenches dangled like sycamore keys from his thumb. My aunt offered to drop me to the train into Boston.

The train was full of Saturday spiritedness. Young parents held children to them and asked enthusiastic questions about what they might see at the aquarium. Did they think there would be a. Who was looking forward to the. Strangers talked about the weather. Two backpackers were told they'd certainly picked their dates. A tropical storm was brewing out there, said an old man, and he waved his hand behind his head as if the sea were in the window. Another man joined in to say he'd heard it all before, it always got downgraded, it was part of weather porn to keep everyone in a state of high anticipation. He goggled his eyes like he'd just witnessed something stunningly wicked on a screen. He patted the backpackers on their humps and told them to have a good one and not let the begrudgers grind them down.

I held on to his bonhomie when I reached downtown. I treated myself to a lipstick at Macy's, fajitas from Fajitas & 'Rita's, and a book about Jackie Kennedy's clothes from a cart in the breezy, brick-walled yard of a bookshop. A man asked if he could take my photo while I was browsing the carts. He said it was because I looked so absorbed, and he needed that look for a photo. I said yes. Then I hurried for the street, sharply lonely and disappointed in myself at having been found absorbed.

My sister once tromped in on her best friend's parents. To all intents and everyone's purposes, the girls had set out for the beach at Liscannor. Something was forgotten, a magazine, goggles, and then the scoot back to the hotel. Rooms with connecting doors. She says they were in her sights before she took it all in. There followed a long evening, dinner at different times, skulking, nothing said to her best friend. But I tugged the details from her like a tapeworm. His hairy back. Soles blacked from sandals. The gentleness and how everything was strangely, wrongly, accompanied by her best friend's mother's caterwauls. In college there was the obligatory walk-in or being walked-in-on.

And there was my aunt, hoiked up on the island. Her legs were slung over Ruslan's shoulders. My aunt had good legs, lean from walking and cycling. Always a little bit tanned. Ruslan was truffling between them. His feet stood one in front of the other. In the race blocks. His hands gripped the brink of the island. He was still in his clothes. Jeans and a navy-blue shirt. The shirt was only a bit slackened, as if my aunt had given up bothering to untuck him and rushed instead to her own skin. I saw them from the French doors. There was no sound. I stepped back and down the steps. I hugged the hedge until I reached the rose bushes. The pink ones were blowsy, ready to be snipped. I took my aunt's private path to the beach. I toed dead crabs and swore at a seagull. The Atlantic didn't give a damn.

That evening Ruslan finished the handrail and grilled trout for dinner. My aunt read aloud a *Daily Mail* story about a boy who'd pretended to be the dead son of a rich family. Ruslan said the deceit worked because the family must've known all along. They were desperate to have their son restored to them. Any son would do. He spoke with the same concentration and curiosity that went into cooking the trout, the capers and sliced lemons stuffed in the belly.

A young policeman, his cousin, had been killed in Ingushetia, he told us.

Hundreds of policemen were being killed by Islamist militants at that time, and his cousin was killed by four bullets. He said his aunt and uncle took in another cousin and named him after their son. They gave everything to that boy, Ruslan said, and he used it all for drugs. Now they were trying to find him in the streets of Magas. They wouldn't stop until they came upon him, Ruslan knew, because that was the kind of people they were.

We read about bad weather on its way. My aunt brought armagnac in tiny glasses. Istanbul, she said, flicking her nail at their gold lace collars. Ruslan went to his room to Skype. His sister, in California. A research assistant, he said proudly. A team making headway into motor neurone disease. The door was shut when I passed by. I wondered if my aunt thought *wife*, thought *children*, but refused to pay it much mind.

On that Sunday morning I asked Ruslan to tell me more about that cousin of his shot by the police. He said there wasn't much more to tell about him, except that he had lived one neighbourhood away from his parents and been a good young man and a large crowd of friends cried at his burial. They were all like him, tall and sad and handsome. He said there usually wasn't much to tell when someone had been good and kind all their life. They left a light trace.

I asked him to tell me about the bad one. The imposter.

Ruslan was punching keys on his new mobile phone. He set it on the island by his coffee mug. He braided his fingers and set his chin on them and looked at me levelly. Why, he wondered, was I interested in that chap. Ruslan was given to Britishisms, and they came out when he was at his most serious. Gosh. A bitter pill. Agog. Tight as newts, he said of drunk roarers on the beach. I pictured a small musty bedroom, teenage posters, a single shelf stacked and bowed by Jeeves and Bertie.

I told him I was fascinated by charlatans. The Pan-Am pilot and the Six Degrees chap. Ripley. Ruslan maintained his gaze and said there was nothing interesting about straw men. He told me I should turn my attentions to real people, their real accomplishments. As with carpentry, he had a way of fixing his final point so it couldn't be tested. I should get out and about more, he said, meet a nice Boston boy or a Harvard scholar. I should enjoy the freedom before I started working again.

It was the working again that vexed me. He thought I was living off the fat of my aunt's coastal home, then, off the stock of her fridge and the quilted toilet tissue printed with little daisies. Since I'd been there Ruslan had taken off each morning in a small blue van. My aunt slipped from the house before dawn, quiet as a black-op. He lingered over coffee, the newspaper, email. We passed things to one another, milk, butter. We were wordless as a long-term relationship. He shaved after breakfast, waved from the van before it rafted downhill. But for all I knew he played Keno all day.

I'd seen those lost souls when I passed by bars and

coffee shops. Old men for whom the counter was home, and the screen of jinking numbers. He rarely came home before my aunt, and he always looked as though he had done a day's work but found time to smooth himself out, because that was the kind of man he was, because those were the standards he held to.

Sunday evening and my aunt went out to meet her friends. They congregated every week, but this week everyone was summoned in special honour of the hurricane. Sandy had gathered strength and was bowling for the east coast. They said it now had an eye. It might not hit until Tuesday morning. It might not hit at all. I fell in love with the word landfall. My aunt threw it to one of the friends, said she'd be making landfall at the restaurant round eight. She left a scarf of perfume in the air. Ruslan watched her from the porch, shouted he would tie back the trellis just in case Sandy showed up overnight. She shouted back not to wait up, she might even stay over at Suze's. There were cucumbers growing on the trellis, he told me, a new venture on her part, and what rotten luck to have them destroyed.

As soon as he got to work I asked him about the civil war in Ingushetia. I sat in a garden chair, thick cotton and wood like a film director's. Had he been involved in any way. No, he said. And yes. Because you had to be involved in a country that small. You couldn't dodge involvement. He cut and tied thread as he spoke. He said I must mean killing. Which he didn't. But he gave money and the use of a shed to two of the rebels. One of them was shot dead within a month of the war. He knew the cousin of a suicide bomber. He said he was glad I called it a civil war, because so many referred to it as an uprising. They got that bit between their teeth, he said, and they wouldn't give the country its war.

The sky was ragged and turning for night. Ruslan stopped finicking with the trellis. He sat in the chair across from mine. He was in angry torrent about uprisings and the Arab Spring and his own Ingushetia ignored. He knew when I stopped listening. He must be boring me stiff, he said, he must have mistaken my interest. It happened to him a great deal. He would one day learn to keep mum.

He sat back dejected. His chair creaked and the cotton looked unsafe beneath him.

I'd gone into the garden without underwear. Under shorts I was bare and open.

It wasn't that I wanted him to intuit it. It was enough for me to know, all through the sermon about Ingushetia overlooked in the grand scheme of the world. I left my seat and walked to his. I took his hand. It was poorly done, a hand sent up a shorts-leg. I had to jemmy things along. He looked upset at where he was drawn. He said it was a mistake on my part and I would regret it. He said he'd done his level-best to avoid any such thing. Even the top of his head felt melancholy when I kissed it.

We stayed there a while. His hand deliberated and did its job until I fawned on his shoulder. He said we should call it a night. He smoothed my shorts and walked me to the French doors. He went back to tying the trellis. I heard him secure the whole thing to the fence. Short dull thuds like sounds inside a box.

Later I heard my aunt's car take the hill. Then a low burr of kitchen chat. Then doors. Later still I strained to hear slats trying to be quiet.

In the early hours of Monday he went about battening the house. The forecast was deadly serious. By then the president had declared an emergency. My aunt conscripted me to make leek soup and a lamb stew before the power went out. She was sick of news-talk about hunkering down, but still we should be prepared. We watched walls of waves on other coasts. Window by window, Ruslan hammered big plywood boards to the back of the house. We watched the sea rush under homes on stilts. We watched people Ruslan called bloody fools tying themselves to piers just to say they'd weathered Sandy. One man screamed into the camera. He wasn't going to let that bitch take him alive!

The kitchen was dull like a cellar. Four triangles of light came through the French doors. Ruslan hadn't enough timber to board them fully. The power stayed on. The lights gave one long hiccup in the late afternoon, that was all. I called my sister and mother. They were full of terminology like batter and storm surge from the nine o'clock news. I told them everything was grand, that Ruslan had storm-proofed the house. When they asked who that was, to say that name again, I told them I had to go.

My aunt and Ruslan went to bed for the storm. They tried to behave like it wasn't inevitable. She said she should get through a backlog of emails, maybe hem the new curtains, now that she had this free time. He went in and out of his quarters, sometimes closing the door and speaking to the Skype entity. It might have been the Skype entity that set my aunt drifting from her laptop to the coffee machine and back, then from the coffee machine to his door with a thick blue mug. The door closed behind her. I couldn't tell if she'd closed it, or he had.

I poured coffee into a mug that said Floating Hospital. I sat at my aunt's screen and went through the open tabs. Holiday homes in Croatia. Her credit card bill, payment accepted. *Marie Claire*'s advice on how to maximise one's best feature. My aunt was vain about her hair. I could tell by the way she tossed or crossly ponytailed it in one hand as though about to chop it off, then dropped it on one shoulder, all forgiven. She had an abundance of hair that somehow held on to its russet tones. I imagined Ruslan liked to drag his big hands through it. I left the laptop for upstairs and I ran myself a bath and I looked for parts of myself. I made a little noise, my mouth pressed to the high bath wall. They wouldn't have heard, all the way down there, far inside the din they were making and trying to cover up.

He was probably a terrorist in Ingushetia, or at least a thug, and she probably knew. He was probably married, with a gang of stolid dark-haired kids. But like my granduncle who willed his home to a younger woman, the painter from Sussex, and caused all manner of acrimony, it didn't really matter when that stranger from somewhere, wherever, put in front of you what you so badly wanted all along.

My aunt stayed cooped up with Ruslan all day long. I got nauseous from soup and stew. I made popcorn for watching television. Now all the talk was about high tide.

Someone said the worst was yet to come. The ominous phrase caught on, and someone said it every ten minutes. I turned on the radio, and its people chirped about high tide too. They sounded ebullient, those radio people, bright and excited about the worst that was coming. They'd been the same that morning, telling one another what they'd made for the freezer and how excited their children were to have a day off.

They seemed happier chatting with one another than addressing a listenership.

A buoy off Cuttyhunk Island recorded wind as high as eighty-three miles an hour. I said the name Cuttyhunk over and over. I found that it was south, near Martha's Vineyard. I researched wind speed. Anything above sixty-four counted as a hurricane. At sea, the air filled with foam and waves topped forty-five feet. The whole sea turned white. Cuttyhunk saw it all.

I thought to go out and see the fuss. I wanted to slip down past the rose bushes and find a sea whipped to white fury. From a triangle of French door I saw the rose bushes flattened like horses had galloped through. Wind was all around the house, and rain. I'd heard things flung, paint cans, branches, but still nothing out there seemed perilous. The back door was a problem, all those battens fixed in place by the dead blow hammer. I'd have to go out by the sheltered front and press myself along the walls until I got to the back of the house. The college crowd who went to Australia had posted photos of mammoth surfing waves before they got sixty-hour jobs. They commented on one another's photos, phrases like hot shit, shit hot, holy shit, no shit. I wanted to stand buffeted by whatever shit hit Cuttyhunk, just to film it, just to put it up for all to see.

It didn't come to that. I was buttoning my phone into a coat pocket when my aunt made a showing. She wore black silk, a cami and panties edged in lace. Her face was miserable in segments, a downcast eye, a line notched more deeply between her nose and mouth. One of her cheeks was red, like she'd been lying on that one all day. She wasn't alarmed to be caught out. Behind her Ruslan's bedroom door was open a sliver.

In spite of being brought low, she was candid. The rest of the night would only work, she said, if I joined. It was Ruslan's suggestion. He wasn't like that, she said, only it was something he'd seen years ago in a film. It might have been Russian. There was a blizzard. A hotel was cut off from the world. A room where a lonely man had gone to drink and coke himself to death. He was joined by two strangers. They knocked at the connecting door and slipped into his room and they all spent the storm together. When the snow subsided, everyone in the hotel was executed, but that was beside the point, according to Ruslan. By then I was sitting on the chair next to his bed. The room smelled metallic and soupy. My aunt was cross-kneed at the bed's edge. She looked bored and a touch embarrassed by Ruslan's speech. His eyes were large on something in another dim bedroom.

He wore a pale blue T-shirt and tight black boxers. He couldn't remember why everyone in the hotel was gunned down. It was a Russian film, after all, and he knew Russia for indiscriminate violent happenings and thoroughly bad lots. But the film's ending was a puff of smoke, he said, a bagatelle compared to the tenderness of those women. They lay either side of that man and comforted him.

The scene felt familiar. I'd seen something like it, minus the massacre. In the scene nothing happened except that a solitary man was kept warm. He was lonely for a wife and a child. Or for a dead wife and a dead child. He was an emigrant who could never return home because everyone there awaited success and all he had was fiasco and debt. Or who'd burned all his bridges after some bad thing done years before.

I tried to remember that solitary man's back story. The en suite gargled. High tide, dark water backing up the gulley traps and pipes. My aunt's hand tapped my elbow like a soft okay. She was behind Ruslan's back, her arm enclosing his chest. I was in front, held back from the bed's edge by Ruslan's arm. I was still in my hoodie and jeans. Soon a hand might come pecking for buttons. I hadn't even taken off my boots.

I dozed in and out. The pillow was plump and sweetly scented, as if he'd been breathing his fruit tobacco into it. I tried to get back to that film. In his film things must've gone on. In mine, nothing but a hand held, maybe a calming word. The bath hawked and spat. My aunt breathed steadily enough to be asleep. I waited for the moment I'd know what happened during the Russian blizzard.

At the Super 7

He sat on the edge of a motel bed, early evening, and watched a film. The camera tiptoed as far as a bathroom door that was slivered open at the end of a corridor. Then the camera stopped still. A bow was dragged brusquely across a violin. Then everything turned to the high-volume silence of a teenager leaking herself into cranberry bathwater. A father tore aside the curtain in a commotion of plastic and rings. He raised her to standing, roaring in the fight with her weight and slick nakedness. She flopped against him like a clubbed seal.

After the film ended in nobody's redemption, he needed out of the bedroom for a while. He crossed the street for a 7–11 and snacks. He found almonds flavoured with soy sauce and sweet and sour sunflower seeds. He got two hot dogs because one only made you want another. He daubed them with mustard, ate them quickly by the payphone.

Outside he watched a man feed a Dobermann a sandwich from a plastic packet. The man opened a second sandwich and set it on the tarmac by the dog's front paws. While the dog gloffed the bread and ham, the man drew a little blue bag of shit from his coat pocket and dropped it in a bin beside the diesel tanks. Then he and the dark hulking dog walked into the neon-stricken darkness. Something in the set of their shoulders and their long ready legs made them look hunted.

He thought to go back inside the 7–11 and call Clara's number from the payphone. The little man might answer. He could ask him about coming over on the actual birthday, Thursday, and again for the party on Saturday. He could hint at a trove of gifts. At the very least he could say he was nearby, looking forward, delighted by the robot on the invitation card, Let's Program This Party! But the little man wasn't likely to answer, and if Clara answered he would have to hang up.

He took his bath at eight to spur the night along. There were punishing striplights on three sides of the bathroom mirror and no good place to rest a toothbrush. The bath was pleasantly long, though. He rolled a thin white hand towel into a cushion for his head and placed a wet cloth on his face. The cloth smelled aggressively of chemical laundering. He wore the oval of soap to a soft coin, washing the drive from between his toes and behind his ears. A small sign on the sink said the Super 7 at Vero was working hard at sustainability, and motel patrons should rehang their used towels if they wanted to help save the environment. He agreed with the impulse, but he knew that by morning the face cloth, hand towel and bath towel would remain damp and hostile, so he piled them in the bath for housekeeping to spirit away.

In the concrete corridor near his bedroom door, a machine

calved loud torrents of ice several times in the night. His window was washed by car lights. There was laughter and loud walking. There was one elated yell through the wall behind his head.

He had first met Clara and the little man when they came through Boston on a trip north for skiing. He held the door of the Plaza, welcomed them both to the hotel and the city, bade her to let him know if she needed a taxi or a restaurant recommendation. They stopped in on their way back to Providence. They stood talking under the outdoor heater, and she wondered if it was custom-made for concierges in the middle of winter. The little man was stoutly insulated in a snowsuit, and he smacked his gloves together as if he wanted to make an announcement. After that it all seemed easy.

He took the train to Providence on Saturdays or Sundays. He went to the little man's soccer games and held Clara's hand in the low rickety bleachers. He ran the wheel knife through huge pizzas. He was given drawings made at pre-school, the little man designating a stormy brown blob as an alien from the planet Vang. He took the last train home to Boston. In the empty upper carriage he listened to the thumping contentment of his heart.

He had not realised how hungry he had been. A sous-chef at the hotel, who had lost a leg in Afghanistan, twiddled his badge and told him he was a man in love, and love was the biggest fucking vocation of all. He apologised for his language, it was the meds.

On the wedding day the little man waddled out dressed

like a croupier. He dispensed the rings as though he had done it in some previous life, like some royal child at court. The small crowd cooed.

There was a party at the hotel. The sous-chef made lobster butter for the shrimp and chocolate ganache for the orange macarons. Nothing was too good for a love story this good.

Clara and the little man moved to Boston, and she took the train to her job in Providence. He wondered if she felt any trace of the serenity he had on those evening and night trains. There was an old-world romance to being in the crush of commuters and holding happiness tightly to your chest. He still felt it when they rode the train to see her friends. They walked home from the station with the little man leading the way. He warned them all the way about lava between bricks holding the day's heat.

What had happened after that was so commonplace it took him a long time to claim it as pain particular and unique to him. Happiness leaked away like air from a slow puncture. He could not identify any one starting point or reason, but during snow that stayed entrenched from December to March he realised Clara was in retreat.

She told him she should never have let it get to that point, but she had kept hoping something would flip back to right. There wasn't anyone else, she said. She wondered if he could forgive her. She would forgive herself in the long run, she said, because she knew she was doing the right thing by both of them.

She did a tremendous amount of talking for herself, for him. She roamed around the living room like an actor who needed to get to a certain spot on the stage before particular lines would come back to mind. At no point did she speak for the little man, who had gone to bed with a plush green python wrapped round his thigh.

The evening she set about telling the little man was lamb stew and chocolate ice cream. The new dog next door howled mortally and the neighbour chastised it every five minutes. Durango. Du-rango. DU-RANG-O! The little man sat back, proud of his cleared plate, hoping for two scoops.

When the little man looked at him for confirmation, he had nothing to go on, nothing to offer; he felt nothing but shame. The little man asked for more ice cream. He asked if there would be a playground in Florida. He asked if his friends could come visit. They were a gang now, he explained, and a gang had to stick together. Clara said she thought they could visit, with a bit of planning, of course they could.

After smoothing aside the little man's clammy hair and listening to those stertorous breaths that sped up just before he plumbed deep into sleep, after turning back the sheet to give him what they called coolth, after lining up the monster trucks, after closing the door, after coming back to open it, after standing at the crack and turning away, he shut himself in the bathroom and cried into the bath towel. He would not let her in. She said she would use the other one. He slept on a towel on the tiles and woke to the little man's toe stubbing his backside and asking if he was dead.

To make the little man's birthday he took the week at the very end of April into the first week of May. Someone else would hold his doors open and hail his taxis and know that tall women in pairs after a certain hour were to be ushered in, no fuss, no notice.

He drove to Florida because he was afraid of flying. He had never been able to forget the biochemical smell of his breath in a cup that one time when oxygen masks had dropped. Also, he drove because there was something retaliatory in the long gesture made from north-east to south-east.

He drove until he reached Fayetteville at the end of the first day. He took a motel on the rim of town, near the huge hardware stores and the car showrooms and the restaurants where the onion rings were greasy bangles piled high. He gained Vero and the Super 7 at the end of the second day, and there he would kill time until the birthday party.

In the course of two days he got asked if he was on vacation. He got asked if he was on business. He got asked if he was married. He got asked for his number. He got asked back home, somewhere nearby, just a couple of blocks, no big thing. He got asked to go for a drive to a bowling alley. He got asked to drop someone at the airport. He got asked to pick a song for the teenagers at karaoke. He got saltwatery when they lined up and gave their all to Bon Jovi, *I heard your suitcase say goodbye*. He got asked mildly, with killer southerly solicitude, if he thought maybe he'd had enough.

Teenagers thronged the Vero sand, leaning like crickets on their elbows. Fathers took toddlers down to the water. Mothers stayed behind under hats. The toddlers wanted in the water. At the first toe they screamed with enchanted hysteria.

There was a couple he saw three or four times during one afternoon. They were elderly, and the woman was unwell. It was in the roam of her head, left, right, around the sand, like an animal studying sparse grass. The man steered her by the arm, proudly. It was not hard to imagine him telling her she was beautiful, every day telling her before they went out that there was nobody more lovely. And she accepted the compliment. But who was this extraordinary man? Why so very good to her?

He brought too much stuff to the birthday party. The theme was Lego. He wanted a gift that no one else would bring, that no one in their right mind would spring for. He looked in the aisles of Toys 'R' Us, picking up one box after another and thinking about how they might combine in one big brickfuck world. It was first thing on Saturday morning and the place lurched with kids looking for the best new thing. He went for the biggest box, Sea Rescue. A stretcher hung from a helicopter. A trawler lay confounded, askew. Ambulances waited on the shore.

Then he added a box of soldiers. Then a hospital. And next to the hospital a pizza place. And an apartment building that would be owned by the same people as owned the pizza place. It might get flooded in a storm, it might burn to a mound of black bricks. He and the little man would spend hours wreaking one catastrophe after another upon this fishing town. In the checkout line a little girl studied all the boxes in his arms, then looked in accusation at her father.

Clara asked him what the hell he thought he was doing, bringing that much stuff. Who in their right mind brought that much stuff? People sent Lego to the orphanages in Romania, he remembered from television years ago, massive boxes of it, tubs and pails of bricks and tiny heads and bits of roof and fence. The lost-eyed kids with legs twisted up around their shoulders loved that Lego. You could never have too much Lego, he said. She told him to set the boxes down in the front room, scattered about so they didn't look like they all came from the same person. He put Sea Rescue standing up on the coffee table. The tableau on its cover shone valiantly blue.

Clara's boyfriend was at the party. He was a personable, fit-looking man, a bit younger. He was constantly moving from kitchen to yard with plates of food for grilling. There were five other couples with kids, and several women in love's disrepair. One of them gave him a small red paper plate of food and asked him how he was enjoying his vacation. One of them gave him her number in case he needed a tour guide. One of them had not let go of the pinot grigio's neck since she joined him on the porch. It was impossible, she said, absolutely fucking impossible to find a good man on the internet. They were all broken from something or other.

In the garden the boyfriend shot at the little man from a big green gun that expelled long foam bullets and water. He seemed livelier in this part, he wanted to succeed. The little man shrieked and picked up the foam bullets and threw them at the boyfriend. Nothing struck. The boyfriend shouted that the little man didn't have a chance and he might as well give up. The little man got more interested in finding the foam bullets than in the combat. When he could not fit any more in his pockets he jammed them under his armpits. He walked to the deck and shed the whole magazine beside the glider. Everyone got busy with cake.

Someone had brought cupcakes. The kids tore into them. Everyone loved how their little faces got smeared red and purple. Everyone bustled to take a photo. He hated seeing the little man made a mug of.

After that it was back to phone calls, once a month, on a Sunday evening. Later, Clara was kind in the circumstances. It wasn't that he shouldn't call, she said, only that she had been recommended to curtail it to holidays and birthdays. But he would be there for the birthdays, wouldn't he? It would not be a case of calling. Was he right? He demanded a read of the situation.

Maybe attending birthdays wasn't the best practice, she suggested, it only served to confuse. Anger teemed through him, a gale of hurt and dread. He said stuff. He cursed her word 'attending'. She handled him off the phone by saying he had no claim, surely he always knew that. He wasn't the little man's dad, but of course he could call on the holidays.

Back when she was as in love with things as he was, he raised the question of adopting the little man. He wished that a derelict father in England could be annulled, swapped for a better one. She smiled gratefully and called him a good man, already the best father there could be. But she told him it was impossible.

The little man's father might one day deign to acknowledge him. She said the little man spent industrious hours drawing pictures in which his father had a smile as wide as something cut into a pumpkin.

*

May again. Another birthday, no invitation. He hit the road anyway. Boston and west. Worcester. Southbridge. Hartford. Meriden. New Haven. Bridgeport. Fairfield. Stamford. New Rochelle. Manhattan. Staten Island. Edison. Hamilton Township. Cherry Hill. Sewell. Washington Township. Baltimore. Bowie. The grim thirst for a beer. Washington. Alexandria. Woodbridge. Dale City. Stafford. Fredericksburg. Spotsylvania. Hanover. Henrico. Richmond. Chester. Petersburg. Roanoke Rapids. General Gau's Chicken for dinner and bed at America's Best Inn and Suites. Smithfield. Dunn. Fayetteville. Lumberton. Dillon. Florence. Walterboro. Savannah. Brunswick. Kingsland. Fernandina. Northside. Jacksonville. St. Johns. St. Augustine. Palm Coast. Daytona. Port Orange. Titusville. Rockledge. Melbourne. Palm Bay. Vero Beach. The swashbuckling light of Florida. The Super 7's calamine stucco.

And they weren't around. Clara's brother and sister-in-law had planned it all, she said when she finally answered after he spent three hours getting voicemail. Disney World, how could she say no? He said he would wait in Vero, he had the time off, waiting was no problem at all. Dinner on their return, he pressed. She wasn't sure.

He spent that week very still on the beach. Two Icelandic girls offered to slather sunscreen on his back when they noticed he was taking on red. He liked the light slap and knead of their hands. If he were another man he would invite them on for drinks. He would test their limits. He thanked them and made a joke about being saved from cancer. One of them said it was not something to laugh at. You can get a melanoma even on your vulva, she said resolutely, nobody should take any chances.

Dinner got moved around twice. In the end it was rewritten to Sunday brunch on his last day. The place was jammed and they had to loiter in line. Families got impatient and cranky on the burned-sugar smell of French toast. The little man gripped a console until it buzzed red to say their table was ready.

When they were settled and massive tankards of iced water brought to them, he asked Clara about the boyfriend. That's on hiatus, Clara told him. The little man was trying to read the word hollandaise. He had turned chubby. There was a time when it seemed he would go to lankiness and angles, and he might still, but that morning the little man had the bready paleness of City Hall men he knew who ate lunch specials at the food courts.

The little man had to be pressed for information about Disney World. He liked Typhoon Lagoon. He saw twenty sick children with no hair. Some man bought his mother Mickey Mouse ears because he thought she would look good in them. She shrugged and said the Magic Kingdom was full of losers.

He needed the table to himself and the little man. Did she have anything to do in town, he inquired, he could hang out with the little man while she did. Clara looked like she was about to say she did, but she didn't. They were going on to a birthday party. Nothing but birthday parties, she said, a racket, the pressure was too much. He asked the little man if he still played with Sea Rescue. He wasn't into Lego anymore, he said, he built stuff on apps.

The parking lot was blistering when they walked out. Families emerged from cars, in fours, in sixes. He told the little man he would call him and he would send something and he would be back and he would tell everyone at his hotel what a good speller the little man was. The little man shrank back into his skin. His eyes got smaller with suspicion. But they didn't know him, he said, those hotel people had never met him.

He could have stood there bracing the weight of the sun on his back, reminding the little man about the mornings he brought him in through the kitchen, where he was kootched by everyone prepping veg and tumbling loaves into crates. That time he bore the little man on his shoulders through the ballroom where they were lowering the chandelier to clean it, where they both lay on the lobby carpet and studied the ceiling's gold pomp and fuss. Your son's a good boy, said the busboy and the chambermaid and the old guy who draped the day's newspapers over wooden batons near the fireplace. Your son's a good boy. He let them say it.

He skipped his last night at the Super 7, drove back to Boston with stops only for coffee and bathroom. At the end of the journey he slept in the car because the apartment would be clean and correct like he had left it. He could not face the truth of its corners.

In the morning a recycling worker woke him. Thought you'd gassed yourself, man, he said, thought I was best to check you up. He said he'd seen it all. Just last week someone tried to throw himself into the path of an oncoming recycler—but it was in Springfield, and they had a lot to contend with out there, opiates, no jobs, hell, he'd go under the wheels himself if it got as bad as Springfield. He rapped goodbye on the window and jumped back onto the truck's running board. The city pressed towards light, slowly, adamantly.

In the following years he came to know where to get a good lunch in Fernandina, and the way to winkle the meat out of crab claws. That there were good bookshops in St. Augustine. That there was one unmolested place for watching sundown in Daytona.

He did not get to see the little man every time. There were birthdays from which he was dissuaded, or prohibited. Once he turned up in the small hours and sat in the car with the lights dimmed, and a neighbour called the police.

Last birthday they were hosted by the boyfriend's family in a fancy subdivision of Port Saint Lucie. Port Saint Lucie had botanical gardens. He spent the whole day there. He watched a tai chi group, their imperceptibly slow movements, some deep knowledge spreading on their sunlit faces. In the evening he watched a jazz concert.

Elderly people rose from their seats and shook their hips at each other. He marked the little man's birthday with a Scotch at a bar in town and went back to Boston the following week.

If Port Saint Lucie was on again, he would go to the botanical gardens again. There were flowers so audacious they should be outlawed, and a little lake. This place wants to be Puerto Rico, said an old man leaning down, stroking pink leaves like they were part of a woman's lusciousness, it wants to be Puerto Rico, but it's not bad at all for something man-made. Do you love these? he heard a woman compel her boyfriend or husband, whose hand was slotted into her backside pocket as though he came with the jeans. She indicated the one called goyazensis. Do you love these? The boyfriend or husband said he guessed not as much as she did. He wondered showily if the flower had anything to do with the Spanish artist, the way boyfriends or husbands did when they needed to win something back.

He would like to lie on the shale at the edge of that counterfeit lake, lie there as the day edged to a dark remoteness. Stay there to consider what next. Then head back to the motel, until time with the little man might be agreed upon, bowling or getting deafened by Dolby at a film, until such time as the little man was the one to say no.

Mavis-de-Fleur

In the time it took her son to schedule a call, she got close enough to love to singe her eyebrows and feel a whole steppe's worth of emptiness when it ended. What else? She had her IUD taken out because its time was up. The gizmo left her during a grim afternoon procedure, the nurse tugging so hard she toppled back to the sink, saying *well wow, some don't give up without a fight*. She wanted to see it, to know if these coils turned verdigris like the roofs of old noble cathedrals, but she didn't ask. And? She watched other expiration dates, cheese and sunscreen and credit cards. She learned about bond ladders and put money there for maturing at different times. She patiently watched many things end or change, all the while waiting for his message, *talk yeah?* and calculating what she'd tell him happened in the long interval. She loved her son like the mothers of fugitive criminals must do, in silent pride, in the nasty secret hope that someone decades hence might turn them in for cash money.

The message came through on an evening she sat in a bistro with her most scholarly, independent friend. They met once a month to catch up. Her friend gave out yards about many things and barely elicited an opinion in return. This time her friend was all shenanigans, though. She had placed a pricey personal ad in the *London Review of Books*. She snapped through the thin pages to display, *Former Queen of Connaught, exile in London, heightened 50s, seeking something*.

I thought the ambiguity might be useful, her friend said. A cliffhanger. That and I'm on a budget. Nine words, not counting the prepositions. You can tell a whole life in that much.

She admired her friend's campaign for high-mindedness and style in an age of the raw and the crude. Her friend was the kind of person who threatened to end friendships if people emailed without capital letters. They went down through the menu and ordered hummus and baba ghanoush, then wondered if puréed things would ever be enough to sate them. They agreed they could always order more.

Her friend had already received a spate of inquiries, before her *LRB* even showed up in the post. She said the emails proved everything she knew of modern life, its thinness in the categories of what mattered, and its desperate, compensatory longwindedness.

They all feel close to the void, she said. They write at length about not winning anymore. They propose a range of outings and activities, and every pub has a name ending in Head.

Her friend dipped her head to the page and read aloud other personals in a mock-forlorn voice.

Would *you* ever, though? I'd help you draft one. Or we could post a joint one. Two Serious Ladies.

Her friend was animated by gimmickry now, and she indicated to the server they'd take another bottle. She closed her eyes and a galvanic shiver passed across her shoulders.

I have it! Ready? Here we go. Two Serious Ladies. Quote. No one among our friends speaks any longer of character, and what interests us most, certainly, is finding out what we are like. End quote.

She sat back against the banquette leather and smiled in consummation.

There. Isn't it wonderful? Jane Bowles'll never let you down. But it might be too many words to be reasonable.

The evening passed in more plates of mezze and tumblers of house red. Several drinks in and her friend's memory dredged treacherously. It always did, dragging up men by whom they'd been burned through the seasons.

Who was that one, the one who took you to Santorini? The baking classes, that same one, that you *paid for* and he couldn't be bothered with laminating the pastry?

She remembered him, yes, and cycling heavy bikes around Hyde Park. In the evening her legs had been heavy and indolent, as if they were the chiefly sexed part of her. So there had been nice times, too.

For the rest of the evening they tore strips off Prince Andrew and other royal fools. When she took out her phone to send half the bill to her friend, there it was, *talk yeah?* in a blue bubble sent from the seafloor or the sky. She tacked as fast as she could to the Tube, squeezing the phone in both hands, rushing out the sliding doors like a bully. She slipped into her flat quickly and quietly as an envelope and arranged herself at the small kitchen table, phone against the snake plant.

When he came into view he was turned to the side, almost fully around, and astonishing light splashed him from some high window. His hair was white now, and long, where last time it had been pepper-grey and cut in a shag. The white looked better against his pink face, more committed and consistent a colour scheme, but still it was a shock, and her chest worked hard to draw breath and hide her dismay.

Judging already, is it?

His voice was both scratchy and mellifluous.

No, no, she said. You know me. I always get a bit winded at the sight of you. He tilted his head beguilingly.

You've been out on the town, I can tell. Nice jacket. A date?

No, she said. I've decided from now on it's friends and fun.

She told him about the new bistro called Foxtrot and her friend having lost a noticeable amount of weight.

I think she's back smoking.

Sad, he said, though what the word meant, said in that flat tone, she couldn't tell. The light spread suddenly, and she could barely make out his face.

Times of cloud, he said, clearing to sun. Weather app said so.

Where are you, she said, that it's that bright?

If asked on a television quiz where he lived, she would

be so slow, so flailing, that her timer would buzz, the camera pity her, and the topic move on to something less consequential. He never gave answers to the basic questions, location, wellbeing, contentedness. He wouldn't give anything up.

I have a new friend, he said. Check this out.

He turned aside and dropped to pick up something, a dog, a very small dog with a big head and eyes that looked blind.

Another one, she said, deflated, because behind him or nearby were dozens or more. She had seen them over time, singly or in small groups, and proudly exhibited. Sometimes they roughed up the call with their barking or lunging, and she tried to imagine how his quarters smelled. Meaty and fishy, ammoniac with farts.

So, what's that kind, then?

When she showed interest, the calls ticked over longer.

Boston Terrier, he said, chucking the dog under its chin. Temperamental as hell, and don't leave your best suede lying out. But they love a person to death.

As a child he was one of those zealots forever trying to save imperilled creatures. He went about raising money, selling lines, holding raffles. He made rounds on a bike, with an officious little clipboard of literature and imagery. Retriever pups injected with MS, Spanish greyhounds' jaws wired shut. By night she dropped him at gates and sat with the engine running until he jumped in gloried with money or filled with loathing for households that sent him away without a pound or a pledge.

The Boston Terrier's eyes bloomed opal on the screen.

The dog regarded her cursorily, coolly, like assistants in the modern clothing shops she tried but left empty handed and more lumpen.

She forgot what he had studied in college because he never talked about it during holiday breaks or weekends. Her friend reminded her one time. Something involving big data.

That's what it's *called*, her friend said. Big. Data. Caps. And they scrape it. It sounds OB-GYN, doesn't it? But it's not. It's the next big thing.

He had no interest in his degree, he said, no use for it when it was done. When he finished, he needed a place to live, just a while longer, that was all, until his next move. He kept nine-to-five hours in his bedroom and never brought home friends. He wore the same clothes he grew up in, duds in mediaeval browns and greens, a waxed jacket veined dark from no cleaning. And he cared in a less incandescent way about his old causes. In the poultry aisle he merely steered her from the shrink-wrapped limbs and wings and suggested she take on a cat.

For when I'm gone, he said. The company'd be good. You used to like Chivers.

Cats aren't company, she said. They're stalkers. Chivers was an exception.

She heard him moving in the kitchen during his last month, rattling pasta into saucepans and tinkling spoons in teacups. In the end, he stayed all the way to Easter. By May his bedroom was neat and neutral as a soldier's quarters.

How many now? she asked.

Dogs? I don't count anymore.

What's the weather like? she tried.

Outside her kitchen window the street looked lit by animal fat, filmy and trembling and drab. She shifted on the chair, caught in a stitch. The missing copper coil, and however many other contrivances, all adding up to not having had another child.

He asked if she still used the same weather app, the one that used to reach for poetic language, like times of cloud, like nascent thunder.

But by winter it got lazy, she said, didn't it, though? Everything wintry mix, everything.

If he were in that job, he would go full blast for the worst conditions. Milk comes frozen home in pail. Fog as thick as roux.

High probability of lows and depressions, she thought. Some spotting that may be a period, she said.

She used to make those kinds of jokes because she saw it as part of his education. When he was seven or eight, she told him how it all worked, living-room couch, cat on his lap for comfort. What went where, and all the necessary and sufficient conditions. He turned waxy and pale and grabbed Chivers's mother so sharply the old tabby squalled at the assault.

What, he had said then. Why?

She asked if he was reading and writing again. I'm tapping, he said. I'm tapping a bit.

He got out of the chair and spoke from outside the frame.

If I put my mind to it, I could write a biography for each of these little souls.

The camera refocused and she saw dogs and more dogs.

Every time she thought she had a headcount, one left the tableau and a few more wandered in. They seemed content to be packed so closely.

The phone flashed green across the top. Her friend. She pressed red and continued to peer into the heaving hive, fur and legs, every so often an ear.

Forget writing, she said. You should paint them. That's what you should do. They're already a painting, at least it looks like that on my end.

You're funny, he said. Your enthusiasms. We all remember the time you said no way to getting a dog for real.

Her stomach tightened to the blow. She hated when that time came up in conversation. And it always came up.

You just wouldn't believe a person could love an animal as much as a person.

That's right, she said. I was way off. Way way.

Her friend again, this time a message. She could read it and keep him on the line too.

Hang on, she said. Fleur's sending something.

You know that was never her real name, he said. She told me one time. It's Mavis. She hated it.

She took the news like an indignity. To have been out of the know all this time.

And here she was, Fleur, of all coquettish names, sending her a text about an *LRB* email.

I might have someone. Or some two. Couple wanting to take me under their wing. Well-appointed in Bloomsbury. Thoughts?

Now the screen was commanded by a pug, its face a dark mask and eyes oozing miserable grey discharge. She took the phone in hand to type.

You could draw them out to see what's what. But I don't want you abducted and murdered.

Her son was back, and she placed him gently against the snake plant. Where to pick up? What to tell? In previous calls she found tedious housekeeping stuff good for throat-clearing, to see if they could go deeper. She told him about the landlord coming in without knocking, with a tablet he said he must use for floor-mapping. He walked around her square feet like a beach figure with a metal detector, hypnotised and determined to hit easy money.

I'm worried, she said. I'm very anxious. Rents are going up without a by-your-leave.

By-your-leave! You're from another century, you are!

And she was, and he was, and they laughed together in the breach.

And the internet, she said, and the phone. And petrol, of course, and gas.

Everything's rocketing skywards.

He told her to ask for a bump at the accountants'. She'd been there for years.

You've become indispensable, he said. What they call institutional memory. If you left, the whole place would crumple.

Fleur-de-Mavis often said the same thing, not to be a fool expecting a surprise promotion. She said she wasn't expecting anything.

And that, Fleur said, is your chief obstacle. The corporate world of men wipes the floor with that attitude.

Here she was again, continuing the Bloomsbury line.

Why do you always go to abduction and murder? Always and ever, with you.

Not always, she said back. *Just a healthy dose of caution.*

I blame that book. The Gift of Fear. In fact, I blame that book for a lot of bunkum. Have we ever talked about that book?

Her friend was so fleet, so funny. It was still frightening, though, to think about what a mysterious couple, that might not be a couple, but one or ten people, might do to extinguish good humour like that.

Hey! her son said. Anyone there?

She had to shut down Fleur or she'd lose the time with him. She said she'd write tomorrow with more considered advice.

Franchement, my dear, I don't give a damn. I just love that word. The French for frankly. A stern one, isn't it! Night, toots.

Did you have many heart-to-hearts with Mavis-de-Fleur, she asked.

Nope, he said. There was only that one time. It was the night you had that sad little party.

True there had been a small soirée, an attempt to bring a few colleagues and friends round her table and see what the chemical reactions would be. After twenty years in London, she wanted to be reflected and passingly known. The one man at the party was from the accountants', always looking for esprit de corps and hoping for love. He went straight to Fleur like a bird drawn south by magnetite. After everyone had drained out the door, his big, worsted coat was the last human likeness, left sleeping it off in the bath.

Was it that sad, she asked? Sad as in pathetic-sad?

Yes, he said, now stroking the long white back of some bigger dog on his lap. You all looked so awkward. And

Mavis was on the run from that big depressive so she took me to the balcony for a chat.

Balcony was a funny word for a French window that opened onto a metal grille for potted plants. Miraculous they hadn't crashed down to the street. They could have kissed out there for all she knew.

Is there a balcony outside your window there? It seems like there might be, with that amount of light.

He left the screen again and spoke at a muffling distance.

Feeding the dogs! Once sec.

Pellets hitting metal, lots of bowls, lots of food.

The party wasn't a big deal, he went on. It's just one of those things a person remembers as disappointing. I was disappointed for *you*.

She asked if he was disappointed now, that she was in the same flat at the same job seeing the same few friends.

I mean, making the usual rounds.

He said at least the bistro sounded new. But, in any case, his disappointment was moot.

It's just not a thing, he said. Not where I am. Nobody around here indulges because what would be the point?

She was getting closer now, hovering to drop a pin on a map. But then it often felt like this.

I worry about you, she said.

He asked if Mavis still liked poetry.

Fleur liked everything that made words work hard. She liked the struggle and was probably now working to craft a response to the Bloomsbury interest. She would get herself in over her head because her words would give a different impression, theatrical, up for experiment.

He remained in the back of the room. The sound of dogs eating dinner swilled round him, percussive and triumphant.

She'd consider a dog if only it weren't too late to be obligated to something new and needy. What she never told him is that she went all the way to a shelter one month after his father left the flat. She went seeking a creature they might get fealty from, and they would, because the whole place smelled of anguish. She went there once a month until something nearly clicked.

She watched a zealous young woman convince a man that pit bulls suffered bad PR.

These days they're called pitties. See the difference?

The man looked remaindered, and the stout dog lunged for his last chance. I'll take her, the man said.

Him, she said. And he's good with children. If that's an issue?

There was no issue.

She watched the transaction moment by moment, she cheered on the outcome. She came very close to taking a mongrel but, in the end, she didn't have faith like that man had, faith in an oddment that might love or eat him.

Mavis recited a poem off the top of her head one time, her son said. Another time, not the party. I won't remember the whole thing. But here. Let me see. One by one they appear in the darkness, a few friends, a few with historical names. Not bad, is it?

Her head was suddenly heavy with envy and trying to keep him on the line.

Not bad at all, she said. Fleur always had good stuff for

the occasion. I'll have to look up the whole thing. Or I'll ask her.

She pressed her eyes hard into her palms and totted up more things to ask him. Were there any other poems she could track down between now and the next time, and did all the new dogs have names? What else? Down in the street, car horns blurted their anger, and someone was kicking or beating a bin. There was panting, too, from the flat above or beside her. More and more young people lived in the building nowadays. Their grocery bags were always small, and they bought bottled water in the big six-packs. They had sex at times she'd expect but exercised in disconcerting off-hours. Their machines crossed her ceiling like a train.

Her phone was black and glassy now. Obsidian, dead hard and precious. The bin continued to take a beating, and now the assailant was shouting too. Some fact of life was being condemned. These were hard times, she agreed, and harder in which to be young than old. Her son might have no hair the next time they spoke, or a rough beard, or a tribe of cats. In all the noise of life that surrounded her but which she never called home, it was time to row away from his darkness. She turned towards the old fixtures taking shape on the coast of the kitchen.

Late Style

The last time I went overseas, the passenger next to me asked if I knew about the plight of the Icelandic pony. It was as if we'd been talking for years.

When they go abroad for competition, she said, they're not allowed to come back. The purity of the bloodline. They might pick up a cold and infect the entire population. Of horses, I mean.

I hadn't heard about it. Was it for real, I asked, with all the advances, inoculation and the like? And if it were true, and those horses could never re-enter, they must long for their own chilly turf. They must be depressed mooching round Wales, or wherever.

You'll make me cry, said the woman. I swore I wouldn't cry on this flight. And now I'm going to cry about your fucking little horses!

Hang on. They were her little horses. She had introduced them, and I told her so. She twisted away to the window. She came back to say sorry. The ponies' predicament might have been true back in the day. She wasn't sure if it still obtained.

I've been on a short fuse, what can I say? I resigned from my job, she said, I sold my house less than market. That's how much I'm not coming back. I love the country but I can't stand the scene. Leonard Cohen.

When it came time for me to leave this country forever, the logics of travel were blasted and I made many tries and false starts. On one call my wait time was eight hours, so I mixed and proofed and baked a loaf of bread and read a short novel in which an Austrian man lived his whole life in one hundred and sixty pages. I had just gone back to reread the most heartbreaking part when someone answered my call to say they couldn't put me on the route I wanted. But there was another, involving four stops and three airports, two of which were in the same city, which I could thread by taking a taxi, as well as a fee in the five hundreds for having to pass like an apparition through the bigger of those airports. The man on the line sketched the route optimistically, saying travellers had made the trip just fine.

A bit tired on the other end, but hey!

He said all was forgotten because they got to where they most wanted to be.

I said no, I would try again tomorrow, and I did, and the next day. And during and around all those calls I worked to cut off old connections.

The old connections weren't too many and my circumference was limited.

Everyone's circle had shrunk. Henry James said real-life relationships didn't simply stop dead, but a writer could draw a selfish circle and decide what was in and what didn't matter a damn. A writer could make it look like friends and lovers fell over cliffs and were done with. It was callous, but truer now of life than of books. A person had to fight to keep familiar faces in mind, and I hadn't. I felt more bereft of books I boxed for the library shop than people I hadn't seen in years.

So I got a more chestnutty colour for my hair and sent text messages to people in cities and towns. Friends and colleagues, people I'd left for jobs in other cities and towns. We had all done the due diligence of trying to stay in touch, until one month became six, one brutal heatwave the next year's polar vortex. From there the years piled up like dense galactic time. We were growing older and more wan, like endives or the fat Belgian asparagus. I still wanted their approval, all of those people. I wanted them to know I'd done well, or fine, or tolerably. I might still do, given time.

I gauged their interest in getting together online. Nobody truly got together that way, I said, though dating and teaching and counselling were getting accomplished in LowBlue light. Most of them responded, but they didn't know the urgency. They said they'd love to, asked to kick it forward a week, were so glad I'd gotten in touch. My hair turned out like goulash, but I kept washing and rinsing until it toned down to something less alarming. In the end six people wanted to get together soon. Open to any day of the week, any time, they sounded avid as the unemployed or the broken-hearted. None of them knew the others. Still I scheduled them all in one meeting.

At five in the afternoon I sat at the screen and waited. My posture was healthy, my distance from the screen approachable. I'd gotten used to working remotely. The word had northerly extremes. I could set up a syllabus in the boreal forest or run a meeting on an oil rig. Remote work simply called for honourable perseverance and the well- timed gushy routine. It meant being the first to flick into action. I was a light in an office block stairwell and I longed for the bulb to pop.

I waited for the shivering light of six people's entry. They materialised, cautious, hopeful faces in good light and bad. There were glitches and hesitations, apologies, logging out and back in. Some were more practised and looked straight ahead like friendly newscasters. Others hunched and gazed down, the screen a missal being pored over.

I had seen some of these people only last year. In other cases world leaders had been and gone. Someone looked younger, someone dejected. My sense of occasion was waning. But here they were, thanking me once more for reaching out. They peeped coyly left and right, birds in the apertures of a dovecote.

It was my job to take an axe to the frozen sea. So. Had anyone read Agatha Christie lately? I said she was forever gathering strangers in a house or on a remote island. It took them days to figure out the reason for being there, but by then it would be too late. A body on the shoreline, another in the dumbwaiter.

Once I got going it was hard to stop. The ice might re-form. They looked at me in dumbfounded amusement and I rattled on. Sometimes it turned out that a few of Agatha's characters weren't strangers at all! They knew one another in sinister ways, unspeakable events stemming from years before. So. Had anyone guessed why they were here? I rolled back in my chair. On screen my smile was lopsided and my left side always my worst.

Why aren't you doing this for a living? one friend asked. I mean, seriously. You could. Are you?

Yes! Yes, another chipped in. It's just like a podcast or something. Rescuing the classics and putting a new spin on them. You should be.

The two people I knew best were in the same trade but didn't know one another. They started speaking at the same time. One professor stopped, the other waved her on, please, please. I was untalented in this decorous warmth. I associated it with people who'd been curated for success from their potty training to their PhD. Please. No, please, you go, they insisted. Me, I trampled others to get to the line, afraid I wouldn't get to the end of my thought.

It's *so good* to see you, said the professor who'd been yielded the time. What has it been, five years, more?

Three, I said. But remember. They were bad.

I would work to keep my remarks short in this meeting. Let others do all the talking.

The other professor said I looked great.

You look younger! I mean, you always looked young. But now you look younger. How can that be? No fair!

This spurred the other professor to ask what I was eating and doing for exercise.

Everyone leaned in for further inspection. I was a buffet item, diners poking round me and wondering about my components.

It's gluten! I mean, it's not. You've cut out gluten.

The first professor said nobody ever regretted getting rid of all their wheat.

Except in those world-building games where it's the next best resource to bricks and ore.

The second professor asked me to remind her of my age. She said she had recently co-authored a paper on women and ageing. *An Objective Hermeneutics of Hotness.* A detour from her usual field of endeavour, but a whole lot of fun. She said she came out of the project determined never to dissemble or disguise when it came to her age.

Okay. Let me see, she said.

She slipped her glasses down her nose and back up.

Hmmm. Forty-five?

I made a greater-than sign with my thumb and finger.

No. No. I refuse to believe that. You're not in your fifties.

I didn't say I was *in* them, I said. I'm not deep in the thicket. But I am over the threshold.

Two people still hadn't spoken. One sent a chat message to say there were sound problems. The other relented and said it was nice to be asked to this. He used to want to be a lover at one time, and he still sent a birthday message at exactly nine in the morning on every turning of my year.

And what is this, exactly? Hi, everyone, by the way!

I said I was leaving the country for good. The jig was up. Fifteen years. They wouldn't have known, I said, but I'd always had my limit set. A woman on the radio said she took stock in year five and really made an audit at year ten. But by then she was waist-high in paperwork and memorising the thirteen original states. It was too late for u-turning when you went that far down the Pike, she lamented. The radio presenter tried to rally her, asking her for the two longest rivers in a cheery, Saturday voice.

I heard that show, one friend said, the first to the podcast idea. I answered the Mississippi but forgot about the

Missouri. Hey, wait. Don't you have the Tombigbee down there?

Sort of, I said. I flow into it at a certain point.

I was asked about work from here on out. I said my institution would let me work out my contract remotely. I'd be doing the same old thing, just at a six-hour time difference. They were pulling back my health insurance and rounding down the retirement contribution. I sounded tedious, like a documentarian narrating labour abuses. Still, attempts were made to tackle my news as though it had some vital import.

That's not too bad. I mean, I don't know how academia works, but that sounds civilised. Is it?

We will always go back to the sea. JFK.

I keep seeing academia called academe. Which is it?

But someone keenly wanted to cut to the meat. Why was I taking this step, after all this time, just when things were slowly turning for the better?

I thought of the hailstones that all the ballsy storm-chasers compared to golf balls, baseballs, bigger balls still. The mobile homes dismembered by tornadoes. Instead I told them about the graveyard on the edge of town. It was called Memorial Park and had knee-high stones and no significant trees of any stature.

That's not where I want to join the shades, I said. I'm leaving the country and heading home.

Their screens clouded over.

Everyone's been thinking like that. Who'll be responsible for my decline and disposal. But for goodness sake. You're nowhere near.

That person, the deferential professor, looked left, smiled at a person or a pet nearby. Then back to the screen with full concentration.

If you and I were talking one-to-one, I'd be telling you this sooner. But no time like the present moment and a bunch of total strangers. So.

A head and shoulders joined her, got too close to the camera, filled the screen with stubble and collars. It was the colleague I used to call And Its Discontents. He was forever tacking that phrase on to topics and thought.

Yes, she said, tilting her head on his shoulder. We're engaged. Re-engaged.

He lifted her hand closer to our eyes. A green scarab ring. He kissed the beetle and wrung the hand awhile. Years ago they had been married in a manner that nobody had fully realised until they divorced. And then it was a public duel to the death every day. He took to wearing cravats and ascots. My group of online guests suited this man.

Now he took both her hands and kissed them separately. Then he kissed each finger. I prayed nothing more was to come, no sucking, no Round and Round the Garden like a Teddy Bear. People were sitting back now. Somewhere popcorn was on the hop. I was still emcee, though, and I had to keep the show going.

I wanted to say goodbye from this end, I said loftily, rather than notify you from the other.

She hasn't heard from you in a year. A year. And she has tried. And now you bring us on, on here, for this dog and pony show?

And Its Discontents was stung and he caught on like contagion.

Very true, said the first professor. I'm not sure what you need from us. Everyone's burned out being online and trying to cope.

The would-be lover cleared his throat.

This. Is. Weird. And I've been to funerals this way. And weddings. I've taken cooking lessons. All of that was weird, but this is just weird.

The tiles were flipping against me. I found the ones that knew me best and threw myself on their mercy. I asked about their wedding plans. That beautiful back garden, maybe? They'd always loved to host.

They were clever, anxious people who used to plan potluck dinners. They persevered even when nobody brought anything tasty or pricey. Blueberry beer, the rubbery wrappers for spring rolls. Kitchen paper for cleaning up after. Nobody ever stayed to help.

And Its Discontents moved to the moment. His wine balloon visible now, he struck it with a pencil and said remarriage to the same person was like an artist's late style.

The idea of surviving beyond what is acceptable and normal. Adorno on Beethoven's later work. Disharmonious, catastrophic even. And thus modern! Here's to my dear disharmony!

He turned to kiss her ear and raise his glass higher, closer to us all. And to whatever else you're all on here celebrating!

I had attended their first wedding, invited because I was new to the country and collectible. The bride's father drank small bottles of Japanese beer and watched all the clever, anxious people get very familiar with the open bar.

All night he watched them like a hunter's dog waiting for birds to drop in the wetlands.

The re-betrotheds huddled even closer together now. They gazed out winsomely, like shelter animals who needed to get adopted together. Maybe I had done something valuable here. An unexpected, possibly hopeful event had come to people's attention. I was ready to end the call on this note.

Someone's background changed to a hovering fog in which kitchen cupboards dissolved. People touched their necklaces and their collars. Someone parted their hair from left to right. Children in framed photos looked fat and thin and extra-terrestrial, and lassitude was gathering. My eyes looked droopy, in need of serum cold from the fridge.

The would-be lover tried again. He asked me to summarise what had been going on in my life since last we spoke or spent time.

I take it back, he said. Not summarise. Synopsise is a better word, don't you think?

He was sending out beams of old longing and I had no choice. The synoptic gospels, I said, to keep things ticking over.

That doesn't come from the same word, he said, burrs in his voice like a knife halfway to sharpened.

And Its Discontents rumbled to be heard.

The synoptic gospels! The Jesus in those three texts is wooden compared to John's guy. Now *he's* kooky and mystic. I call him Lennon Jesus.

This released people to wind down.

We could stay on here all night, I said. The hard kernel

of the party that refuses to crack. It was lovely to see you all.

When God is set to close a door, someone jams their foot to hold it ajar. And a new member joined the meeting. An old friend who'd texted that he couldn't make it but had good reasons. The first thing I saw was how thinned he was. His eyes were wintry, his shutters coming down.

Don't worry, don't worry, he clamoured. Hey, everyone. I've had my liver out and a new one fitted back in its place. If you're wondering, the pain feels like the weight of Australia.

I said the Irish bardic poets used to put slabs of rock on their stomachs to slow them down enough to focus on their art. The pressure, the solitude, I supposed.

I don't believe that, he said. Still, though. Buddhist monks in training were known to sleep on stone or wooden pillows. They woke up many times in the night to meditate.

He jabbed his thumb into his pillow.

This thing, though. Filled with foam. Nuggets fall out every day but I just can't find the hole.

It was a lousy pillow. It was a lousy room. The stuff of care and cleaning was tubed and lumped all around him.

I said I'd send a pillow. Two.

They don't let anything in, he said. They're fanatical about foreign bodies.

Your little star struck innuendos. And Its Discontents sang in low barks. *Inadequacies and foreign bodies.*

Wait, my thin friend said. Wait. I know it! No. I don't know the song. But I know it's Van Morrison.

He sat back satisfied and gained some height against

the feeble pillow. He said I was exactly the same. I peeled back hair and showed roots, I squinched my eyes to show all the lines. When he laughed it seemed to hurt him blissfully.

That's not my point, he said, his voice smoothing out, his chest settling under the covers. I didn't say you look the same as ever. You just are.

Only two others looked like they believed it. And Its Discontents tilted things by giving thumbs up. Nobody could leave in good conscience because the new arrival's cheeks were promontories, the skin polished and raw. He was hungry for an audience. I bet he finally looked like one of his uncles I'd heard about sporadically. They had wine cellars dug into dark hillsides. Their wives died more than they did, and suddenly, and young.

When I said I was leaving the country, he said he already knew.

Like a bolt of blue from the sky. I knew. I just did.

He asked if we knew the ancient Greeks didn't have blue. He wondered why he was thinking of it now.

It's thought they couldn't see it because they couldn't make it as a pigment, he said. They were sure of red, though. And yellow and white and black.

I was wearing my reds again, and he was glad. And the Greeks would be glad of my red.

So the Greeks were colour-blockers, I said.

I pulled my turtleneck up and over my nose.

That's not a bad look, Monte Cristo, he said. You have the eyes to carry it off.

He turned us towards a big window. He told us to look at the magnolia.

It's as old and tall as a ship, he said. This place has a lovely vista. Even when I see the things in the trees. The pills, don't you know.

He shied his head, as though listening to beautiful, heart-shaking music.

Donne sur, he said.

One of the professors sailed in.

Gives on to, overlooks, looks upon, opens to, she said. French is such a generous language. I wish I knew it better. I wish I could return the favour.

We were gathering carefully round him now, with anything we knew and could contribute.

Pillow sham, someone noticed. The stupidest of all household décor.

The pillow sham was quilted and patterned with autumn foliage. New England, long drives through tannic light. Small, self-contained towns and an unfriendliness that was still somehow reasonable.

Who needs this? He hauled the pillow out from under his back and worked off the pillow sham. Who needs as much stuff as this?

We'll need the shams to trade with zombies when they come, I said. They love all that chambray crap.

If you go on a road trip any time soon, he said, at least get a dog, he said. At least grant me that. The company. And not beside you, either. In the back. With the seat-belt designed for dogs. Because if it's a big dog, and you hit the brakes, Buster goes sailing forward and breaks your neck. Think about that.

For someone who never learned to drive, he knew some useful protocols.

Where am I travelling, anyway, in this picture? I asked. And Buster is an inadequate name.

I don't know, he said. I don't care if you're only driving around the block or to another county. That's what you call them, isn't it, counties? Woman and Dog in Car in County Blah at Twilight. I can see you in it.

It was dark at his window by now, and the magnolia loomed like a galleon. His eyes were lit with dark mirth and exhaustion.

I told him about an alert sign on the interstate. Missing Senior. 86, Last Seen Driving a Yellow Honda.

Yellow! That's a full-fledged person that can't be contained. Go him!

I worried the story ended in the Honda gone into a tree, its wings folded round the valiant senior.

The one who needed love and recognition conjured a different road trip for me.

If *you* were a missing senior, you would make it all the way to a bright beach city. I know that about you! No stops for gas and snacks.

He was dreamy in his storytelling, his head cupped in his hands.

Hey. Hey, now!

It was the professor who dabbled in hermeneutics.

She's neither missing nor a senior.

I gammed on for a moment, waving to everyone along the coastal roads. I said I would excel at being a missing senior because I'd make sure not to be found.

That is kind of sad.

She was back, more loudly, the friend with mic problems. She said it was horrible to think of anyone being missing and not being found. Her eyes were dim with concern.

I worry about people, she said. I worry about all of you, and I don't know you. I worry about all the people you know that I don't know.

The friend on the hospital pillow brightened with interest. *Ooh*, his eyes said. *We've got a live one here.*

And Its Discontents honoured her anxiety.

That's perhaps your pure altruism coming through. The concern and wish to aid complete strangers. Most people are reciprocal in their dealings. Like, what does this gain *me*?

He was holding his wine glass askew now, close to capsizing, and his gallant lady brought it back to rights. I'd forgotten how subtle, how elegant a person she was. Some of us got a few short grabs at grace, others held it all the way through.

The friend who worried about everyone said she didn't want to help strangers, per se. It was just that she thought about them more than she used to.

That was my cue. I wrote a private message to the hospital.

Let's not wait so long the next time.

He bopped back at top speed.

Maybe next time I'll have a few cute kidneys to show off!

There was an air of reluctance to call it an afternoon. Because of the high narrow bed and the medical machinery's little red lights, it seemed we were leaving someone to the empty room Blaise Pascal said no man should be afraid to sit in alone. Yet he was and I saw it. I sent another note.

I hope whoever's changing your catheter is getting something out of the transaction.

You! You haven't changed! Actually I've promised him all the martinis I'll never drink again.

While I was laughing and crying and explaining nothing, I was thanked and wished well and bade farewell. Everyone said it was nice to meet everyone else. Then, like items from a magician's tablecloth, they all went away.

I made tea and put away things in the kitchen. I tried to count off everyone who'd spoken. The night was cooling and quieting round me. Someone hadn't. Or had they? One spring I counted the whip-poor-will's cries, in that off-hour when the sky gets marooned between dark and light. I was new to town and trying to learn. My tally was seven hundred, though I heard the record ran to a thousand.

Then pipit, pipit from the front room. The laptop. Someone was budging around, huffing, speaking to themselves in little bird-like bleats. My friend in the hospital. He was moving his sheets as loudly as paper, trying to find the one cool, comfortable spot everyone knows to be there. I stayed behind the lid to listen to his feedback. Anything could happen next. Believing themselves unseen, unheard, people did rash stuff during lulls in their online meetings. I waited for an indiscretion. I loitered until I heard his name spoken by a nurse who wanted nothing but ease and relief for him, who maybe even loved him. I stayed up late until his room fell fully into silence within the full and sumptuous darkness cast by magnolias. I stayed in my chilly front room at a meeting I hadn't left or ended.

S'addipana

The second-born is flying from a burning place to a freezing place and having trouble convincing his boyfriend he won't die above or in the ocean. Perth to London is close to the top of the list of longest continuous flights in the world. And it's not even a straight line, which his boyfriend especially condemns, because this is the twenty-first century, the century *after* the century of aviation. It's a parabola! Or an ogive. Or one of them. Anyway. It's insane! His boyfriend is fairly new, and he is in love. And young too, a Gen Y infantry trooper, anxious about the long-term prospects of the world as a whole and this relationship at a granular level. Together they look at the flight lines on a map. A performative action, a prayerful research trail the second-found useful in the years he did so much travel for work. With that many flights spinning webs round the world, why would his little pond-hopper, his Boston-Shannon, his London-Chicago, be the one frail craft to fall from the sky? He tells none of this to his boyfriend and instead they pan from Perth to London, from London to Reykjavik. As if all that flying time is not bad enough, his boyfriend scolds, let's look at the layer map, shall we? His boyfriend has studied the layer map several times by now. The screen becomes an immense stretch of seafloor topography. I feel like I feel sick, his boyfriend says, leaning spellbound toward the screen, magnifying the ridges and valleys and seamounts, Indian Ocean, Arabian Sea. The second- remembers the word sublime, how a professor of his years ago defined it as a condition of first being awestruck, then feeling ready to throw up. I feel totally sick, his boyfriend says. I should be going with you. This is the twenty-first century. I don't know why it's just siblings sans partners.

The third-born, on the group call they manage to schedule after weeks of trying and getting time zones wrong, her face impassive as a statue on the screen, no chance of getting a word in for a long while, finally gets to say, Remind me, why are we going to Iceland? They remind her that at some moment years ago the first- had suggested a holiday there and everyone else agreed. Why not, they had said to the first. If you vouch for the place, and there's enough stuff you liked there, then it's as good as anywhere the rest of us haven't been. Then followed the caveats. Did they not mention Belize another time? Why not somewhere warm, where people could drink cocktails on sun-loungers and get in and out of the pool like alligators indolently cooling in the depths and popping their eyes over the meniscus every so often? The third- reminded them that those very factors were on offer in America but they had never taken her up. In spite of the weather and the pools and the house she owned, not one of them had come to stay. It's America, the first- had said, what more can I say? The second- and fourth- added notes of disquiet. They chorally disliked her location and would wish her return to Dublin or at least try the other places they lived or had lived in. But the third- has two jobs she likes, and three dogs she loves, and a lover in the second phase of trials. So she's not up for re-rooting. She teaches an art history class once a week at a college haemorrhaging students to better colleges. She tutors painting to princely children whose parents want the best college odds. She shows her dogs at shows because they're triplets from a famous sire. Her lover asks her to bring his sleeveless lumberjacket to Iceland, demands that she wear it in the bleak and rugged territory. He makes her feel old and young and foolish and anonymous, and in that he is like America.

The fourth-born hasn't been on an airplane in years and is taking the long way round. This involves a ferry from Dublin to Liverpool, a train from Liverpool to London, a train from London to Hamburg (changing in Brussels and again in Cologne), a train from Hamburg to Hirsthals (changing in Odense and again in Lindholm), and a ferry from that northern tip of Denmark to Seyðisfjörður in the northeast of Iceland. The ferry will take three nights. Online says you can bring your own food to the bar and enjoy it, no hassle. Then there's a bus from Seyðisfjörður to Egilsstaðir, then to Akureyri, and finally to Reykjavik. He will grudge taking a bus from the airport and walk the last part, the street to the hotel they've agreed on because it offers day-long trips to the famous must-sees.

None of them wants to drive around the country, which the fourth- knows is code for everyone wants to be able to drink whatever they want until whatever needs drowning is drowned. In spite of all their efforts to grow up, away and apart, whoever's the first to crack and get drunk will be tended and loved and asked to pass the bottle tout-suite. The second- says his flight itinerary must surely be more carbon-friendly than the fourth's many conveyances. The fourth- disagrees. He has done the study and the arithmetic. He tells the second- that flying from Perth to Reykjavik is truly unethical, prize-winningly so. You take the biscuit, he says. The fourth- believes in slow time and living in the present. The second- worries a little about the weird itinerary culminating in those long black nights on the North Sea. Mugging and murder and storm swells. But the fourth- is enthused and talking about what's light to pack and what's not needed at all. What he won't say is he's giddy with love and the will to see them again. He would walk the whole map if he had to.

Their parents won't be there, but they've pledged to join online. We love you all, their mother says, and we'd love to see you together, but it's just too dicey for us to make the journey at our age. Their father doesn't say much, which each of them, without having conferred with the others, finds ominous and will have to discuss in Iceland. Their parents were always talkers, toe to toe, point for point, but never scoring points. They had a pleasing choreography that nobody noticed until it was waning. And now it's her, their mother, in the main. She's the filler-in of gaps, the preventer of silences. She talks in mind-numbing, time-wasting ways about the most negligible of happenings, with many, many more details than anyone ever needs, dates and times and lists, prescriptions, soap operas, water rates, weddings, sales, clothing, farming, and occasional, expected deaths. She knows how hard she works, of course she does, and how her children can't wait to get off the line. She knows because the protectors always do, when so much of the act lies in making the shield look seamless. She has read it in a book and seen it in a film, but in both cases the protector was the husband, which she thinks was designed to break people's hearts even harder, just as she remembers decades ago how her husband always got admired on the occasions he went out pushing one baby or another round town. He's marvellous, women used to tell her, he's a marvellous, modern man, I wish I had the likes! Of course they did because he was gorgeous. He speaks to their children now, at last, when everyone's attention is dwindling and lies are being told about battery percentages. Reykjavik, he says, is where Gorbachev met Reagan to talk some peace into him. My daughter's in a photo outside the house. And off he went to find it. The rest of them have no reply, until someone saves the day by saying they'll all go there, to that very house, see what it's all about.

The second- drinks his way to Iceland, commencing at an airport bar with a stinking big gin and tonic. The bartender offers to double it for only three dollars more and it's daft to say no to the cost-saving. His boyfriend will have left the parking deck by now, after checking mirror and shoulder for any remaining signs of the tears he splashed at security. The second- had wanted to get a shuttle to the airport, said there was no need to head out in the car, but his boyfriend said not to worry about the car, the car would be fine. Point taken, said the second. Point of the arrow, tip of the sword. The drive was taut and gloomy, his bag in the back seat like a hostage being moved by stealth and silence. His boyfriend had repacked it piece by piece, some stuff making the cut, other items replaced by items more sensible to weather and terrain. I am in all things a lover, he said, holding up a horrible cagoule, and this sometimes means the tough choices: N.O. And because the second- repacked in the early morning, risking the front pocket for twelve condoms he'd situated flat as a belt, he's drinking his way to Iceland. They won't be used, but it seems important to travel with them, to remind himself he has remaining options, even as he knows he is loved and wanted and missed and waited for. He can hold these opposing ideas in mind and continue to function, just as he can drink gin to open the proceedings, wine to wash down the flight food, beer for its first racy breath from the bottle, and whiskey's hostility the closer he gets to the country the first- recommended. The second- raises a glass to the first-, and it must have been turbulence, his wobbling hand, that had the elderly woman next to him placing her fingers on his knee and saying, There, there. He answered, We're not alone, are we? And she said for the most part she didn't think so. But sometimes, she said. Yes, sometimes. Now that's a thought, isn't it? Her fingers were weightless as smoke.

*

The third- rolls her lover's fat jacket between her head and the window. Hers is the shortest route, ten hours, connecting through Chicago where she's been told to speed through two terminals. Her hands still smell of corgis after ruffling the triplets at lunchtime and leaving them with a student who planned, she said, to paint their royal portrait. Her lover offered to take the train to the airport with her, but she said no need, and he said no offence taken. She knew he knew she preferred him in the established places because he is, after all, a temporary companion. When the settings get confused, like a neighbourhood house party where he fondled her breasts on the back deck, she begins to dislike and not want what they have. Everyone on this plane has a secret in a false-bottomed drawer in their heart. It's the thing each person takes out and nurses in the moment the pilot lets them know they're thirty thousand feet or forty minutes from landing. Her lover has three children he hosts every second weekend and a home in the grungier neighbourhood near hers, and they all disappear somewhere above Québec. Then the great star early droops in the western sky in the night. A line from a poem, the first- saying it to her on an overseas flight when they were in their twenties and in search of white sand and cheap drinks. The first- had lines of poems for all occasions. The third- remembers that they slept the whole way with their heads in dark blankets and when they woke a man was standing in the aisle staring at them, staring almost lethally, until the first said, Please return to your seat, sir. The third- will never have that funny, icy confidence, nor will she ever be stared at like that again, incidental to the first-, as if to stare at both was to learn everything there was to know about the most important one.

The fourth- is sick every few hours on the ferry, unable to keep anything down or close his eyes against the upheaving sea. Everything he was promised has not come to pass. If you weren't a bloke, says an English passenger, I'd think you were pregnant! Get a grip, you're making the rest of us sick. And the fourth- understands, because a glimpse of his vomit, foamy and orange and knuckled with old features of food, makes him throw up again. Here's a fucking bag, fuck's sake, says the English passenger, and the fourth- puts his whole head inside its plastic heat and confinement. From there he tries to think of paintings and films where it's so much worse, Storm on the Sea of Galilee, the Perfect Storm, and then those where tranquillity, once it comes round, can often signal something more terrifying. He has loved and left and loved again and been left, in similar circumstances, all involving the same woman, but everything has been calm for a long time, which makes him wonder. And when he wonders, he can stay on the trail for weeks. He told the first- about this sad pursuit, how easy to follow someone online, and someone's new partner. And she was sympathetic and caustic, which was just what he needed. To hell with the front of their house, she said of a photo of a modern cube, nobody can possibly be happy inside that much glass! Now, his head in a bag, the bag between his knees, he laughs to remember her valiant pronouncement and wishes he'd asked more about her own losses and fuck-ups, which she hinted were legion but which she kept banked offshore. His third night at sea is almost over, and morning moves across the floor and inundates his shoes. Signs of life, says the English passenger, well done! The boat clicks into a spot die-cut for its shape. His vomit has dried to a pancake and he hates the fact that someone else will have to scrub it away. The English passenger steps over it unconcerned, the matter already long past.

Their mother wonders how they're all faring, and who might get there first. Their father says he doesn't know. Who's going? All of them. To Iceland. Meeting up. (She has never been interested in very northerly locations but likes that those places are there to be visited. Iceland has geysers, hot springs and volcanoes. Interesting that so cold a place has that many bubbling, boiling things to do.) All of them? Yes, and travelling from different places, she reminds him. Nice for them, isn't it? (She's not sure when she started to think about what was nice for them without her and him. Maybe a photo from a winter dinner years ago when all of their lines coincided. She had never seen the first- laughing so hard nor the fourth- look so well dressed.) He supposes it is nice. He hopes they'll come back. Will they come back? Of course they'll come back. Well, not all of them back here. And anyway only two of them lived in this house after we bought it. (She'd love to secretly visit the house where they all lived together. If it were for sale again she should pose as an interested buyer and drift through its small rooms, take the wrongly tall step up to the kitchen that all four of them tripped on one time or other, cracked foreheads, a broken nose, the long narrow back garden where they ran and fought and shot the hose at one another, dangerous as police in a riot.) What's on your mind, he says? I was just thinking about the old house. They're never coming back, he says. That's what happens, isn't it? Well, you're right. In the sense that we'll never all live in the same house again. Yes. He says that was the best time. But I liked the time before them, too, he says. And I like now. Do you like now? I do. I have you all to myself. (For that she might stroke his penis this evening and melt him to moaning on the couch. She's always surprised at how half-hard it is at all times. He's always surprised at the outcome, proud, bashful. And in that he hasn't changed one bit.)

The hotel room is small and square, a container in which to scrabble like a crab from corner to corner in search of darkness, but the second- has no such luck. The windows have vertical corporate blinds that don't reach the edge, and that last line of afternoon light becomes all the sharper just before it dies. The second- is the first to arrive, though he knows the fourth- has already made land and is on his long bus journey to reach Reykjavik. The second- doesn't understand such saintly procedures. And no word from the third-, but that's to be expected, meaning she could be coming through the front doors right now or stuck indefinitely in some unplanned city between rerouted flights. You'll hear from me when you hear from me. She's that kind of stoic, whereas the second- is now feeling sick with the need to sleep and rinse his nerves clean. He's sweaty, too, having decided against the shower, same with coffee offered by the sternly compelling woman at reception. She has an angular presence he used to go for when he slept with women, girlfriends his siblings found forbidding or *just not peeps*, as the first- deemed them. The bedsheets are tingly and stubborn, so he looks up things to do in Iceland. And there after the fumaroles, the waterfalls and the whales, someone mentions Iceland's only serial killer and the locations, including his burial mounds, which are three, because his body was cut in several pieces and buried under separate cairns lest he return to haunt the region with his axe. The map's coastline could be the west of Ireland's ragged indentations and belligerent peninsulas. The grisly murders happened in 1596 and there hasn't been anyone like Axlar-Björn since then. The second- falls asleep thinking of the various murderous countries, to a greater or lesser degree, in which he and his siblings live, and why they couldn't find a way to live in one murderous country alone.

The third- is early, but now she's involved in someone's burst luggage at the airport, which means she might be late, depending on how long this altercation goes on. All she did was help a young woman who indicated that the chintz-print was hers, waving, running unnecessarily, for everything comes round again. But she didn't want to let the suitcase take a second run round the track and so the third- lunged and grabbed it for her. The suitcase, in spite of its homely, gentle print, was solid, hard as a boat, and it twisted its bulk off the carousel and fell cracked on the ground. The third- is standing above it and the owner is bearing down. She finally gets what this phrase means, bearing down. Here comes the young woman shouting, cursing lightly, then more heavily when the damage becomes clear. I'm so sorry, says the third-, it cannoned off the side, there wasn't much I could do. You could've left it alone, shouts the young woman, lit with anger and far more energy than anyone else in the terminal, you could've minded your own business! The third- always finds it strange when women attack one another. Strange, only occasionally comical, but because she's jangly tired she might burst out laughing now at the woman who keeps haranguing her next to the body of a smashed suitcase. Her wrath is in excess, but now the third- sees the source of her worry and woe, a beautifully smooth *objet* that miraculously survived the disaster to delve a vagina again. It's the notion of ceramic chipped riskily near someone's cervix that sends the third- over the edge. She asks the young woman what was breakable in her suitcase. Nothing? Good. Because every little thing was fired in a kiln. Fine then, off you pop. And the third- walks to another spot along the carousel and expects her bag to be the last out.

The fourth- is walking to a marvellous church called Hallgrímskirkja, noted from many points on his bus trip into the city. He must see it before the others do. He has so little worldly stock compared to them that reaching the futuristic structure means something, even if that something is competitive and petty. Then the whole thing rises before him like a concrete rocket improbably docked, austere and unwelcoming. He loves and dislikes the immensity. The main church building is tucked behind it like the long caboose of a farmyard fowl. He pledges to come back with the others to see the massive organ pipes and stained glass said to be inside. Still, he will have gotten there first, and in that he feels a bold stab of kinship with Leif Eriksson, who's out in front of the church, high on a plinth like the prow of a ship, booting forward with a long-handled Viking axe and his cloak swelling like sails behind him. The first- had, for a time, lived near Leif Eriksson in Boston, a statue she said was a man-child compared to the guy in Reykjavik. The fourth- doesn't know what kind of people she loved or was loved by during her years in small and big European cities, only that one time she told him, in a voice like something rusty in need of oil, that she'd spent a year shrivelling from and throwing herself again and again at a lover who left her sore for days. Straining on the toilet, she said, feeling adult, of all things, for saying yes to exceptional pain. The fourth- had nearly wept to hear this bleakness and said she should receive tributes and fealty and kindness. He'd take the long weapon from Leif's grip now and exercise it on whoever it was that left his sister in need and hurt, who in the cheap and painful ways of the world probably had no idea that she was gone. People bounce off one another or move through one another, maybe deliberately and devotedly, for a time. Then they move past and well away.

*

Their mother isn't sleeping, but their father is, according with their usual choreography of her going dark first and him staying awake and trying to read a book or the news abob on his phone. The sounds of his being at odds with or confused by the world, all its fires and floods and geopolitical bedlam, reach into her ears and under her eyelids along with the bright and shifting emanations from his phone. All the red flares mean the *Guardian*, hospital white the *Irish Times*. She loves to be woken because it means she can look once more on him before she falls asleep again. If she were a sculptor she could shape his nose and ears with one hand tucked behind her back, the free hand fingering through clay for his nostrils and ear canals. She can lie like this for an hour, more, gathering him, sometimes smelling him, especially his shoulder. Soon enough his phone quiets down to a dark and pond-like surface, and that's always when she thinks of killing it in the toilet. She blames it often, and fiercely, for his drifting, though the doctor scoffs at this and ruthlessly reminds her of clumping plaques. But by all means take custody of the phone, the doctor says to her, if you think it's really a problem. Indeed, maybe you shouldn't have gotten it for him in the first place, the doctor said, and again she felt responsible, as much to blame as the benighting phone and the beta-amyloids. At first he was distracted by the phone, twitching to find and hold it, but soon enough the relationship became continental, he moving with the phone steadfastly away from her. Iceland has plates that she read about, grounds splitting and moving apart so at one particular location you can stand on what belongs to

North America, on the other Eurasia, and both are moving away from each other by nearly three centimetres every year. She couldn't love him more if she threw herself into the rift valley to save him.

The golden strip of condoms sits glinting mediaevally on the high-piled pillows, and the second- knows he will throw the unused eleven away. Their travelling this far was gesture enough, scanning through as solid luminous rings on an airport screen. With an unrolled condom draped across his forehead, he records a voice message for his boyfriend. It used to be that the app cut recordings at thirty seconds but now it goes far longer, even when there's little to say. For example, he's here, which his boyfriend will already know from tracking the flight. And the hotel is nice enough, which is true of most waystations he has stayed at for work. And the jet lag might be weird, given the strange length of his journey, but it hasn't set in yet. He could say he's uneasy about the arrival of his sister and brother who, as far as he knows, are wending their way to the city right now. He could add a note of disappointment in the city, at least what he's seen of it, because all it looks like is a nice enough market town. Now the rubber is clammily alive and he moves it in the other direction, drops it vertically over his nose. When the message comes to its natural end, which is his summative effort to make Iceland banal to his boyfriend, he stops recording and draws the condom into his mouth. Around his tongue it tastes not anywhere as pungent as it smells. How long could he keep it in there without gagging and swallowing? He is fifty-two and more suffused with sadness than he has ever been in any other decade of his life, except perhaps the one during which his mother and father moved him and the first- to a new house and the new school where he was treated like shit on a shoe for a year. He expels the condom in a little bin by the desk. He hasn't cried in front of his boyfriend, but he did at the dentist's, inside the hard-edged goggles, and she thought the drill had gone too far. No, he said, not nearly. And he hacked out a laugh to let her know he meant it and he didn't.

The third-'s skin prickles with recognition of something in the air of the bus. Old perfume fallen down to a powdery note, very like what the first- wore to define herself. Chypre, she announced on buying her first oil at the age of fifteen. Body Shop, best friend, bus to the city and back. She brought wrist to nose every few minutes and looked transformed by what she breathed. The third- tried a dab from the little plastic bottle but it didn't give her the same delirious pleasure. And it was the oaks and mosses from then on, the first- never going anywhere unscented. Chypre was part of her fluent style, in clothes and shoes and hair, and the third- was uncouth in comparison, always trying and rarely winning. Those years were edgy with jealousy and admiration, and the third- would go back if she could. The chypre-smelling bus is half-full of lone travellers, and half of them are dozing. The Icelandic road goes through landscape flatter and far browner than she expected, with dark gravel everywhere glinting on all the verges. She could be on the way to a nuclear reactor or a prison complex, the route so commonplace and alienating. Strange choice, her lover had said, but he was quick to say he heard good things from people who chose the stopover option on their way to elsewhere. He expressed interest in the volcanoes, of course, of which there were dozens, some sleeping and some bubbling beneath the surface. Strange choice. He didn't know about the first-'s fondness for the place, and he didn't know a great deal about anything in her family because she had sustained a cool, need-to-know clause after he said he didn't feel right, indeed ethical, about talking about his children to her. She insisted they avoid the weeds of other demands and attachments, and this will make it easier to draw things to a close. The outskirts of Reykjavik take shape around her in utilitarian buildings and dawning signs of coming attractions.

The fourth- waits at the desk until someone comes through a door he hadn't seen concealed in the wooden wall. It's a modern wall and the receptionist has modern geometric hair that rests in smooth pale wings against her face. He's been waiting so long he hadn't thought anyone would come, he tells her. And she says, of course someone would come, for someone not to come would be unheard of. Her words are steel-cut and surgically healing. For someone not to come would be unheard of. They are so perfect and he is so tired that he turns away in tears. She sees this but doesn't ask him anything, simply turns to the screen and says his brother checked in a few hours ago and is probably asleep. Australia, she said. He came all the way from Australia, which most of our guests do not. And you, she asked? The fourth- says he came from Ireland but took the long way round. She takes his credit card number for incidentals and tells him his brother is on the same floor. Are there are more of you coming here? And he can't stop, though he tries to stifle it. He bursts out laughing in the most helpless, passionate way. Any more of you, as though she expects an army of extraterrestrials or local militia. It's much too funny, funnier. He apologises and says their sister is coming from America. Now she's really peering at him. Australia. America. She suspects some form of terrorism, or at least criminal intent. I do not understand, she says. I really do not. Her smile is quite lovely, and if he ever started to think about making sexual overtures ever again this would be the first woman he would choose. Australia, she says again. America. And you, I will call you Ireland. It doesn't stack up well against the other two immensities, but still her voice is affectionate. He says that is totally fine, she can, he would answer. Now it's time to get some sleep, she advises, and gives him a cardkey warm as a secret from her hand.

Clock chirping. Snoozing. Chirping again. Their father wakes to their mother's alarm and unfixes the little clock from where she holds it like a bird between her hands. He feels fresh, washed, from the night's sleep, and goes down in pyjamas to make tea. The dog is snoring like a drunken nun. Winter light fills the sink with bright ferocity and floods the black counter. Mornings in the kitchen are for thinking big and small, before his days exact their dues in things to know and do. The kettle boils with bubbling blue light. The whippet raises an eyelid at the sound of cups. Rascal. Rascal. Rascal. His first- got them the whippet from a friend with a litter of six when everyone agreed it was time they got a new one. It already had a name because the friend loved Russian literature. Raskolnikov, but that was a murderer's name, his first- said. Not a good idea for a dog, could give him great and dangerous notions. So, Rascal. The whippet comes to twine round his leg. Of all the threads he needs to hold, his first- is the one he puts most work into. Never pulling too hard for fear she might slacken or snap. He knows an Italian word for this because she told him. S'addipana. That's Montale, she said, and all translators say it's hard to get right. A thread is being unwound. Being lost. None of the translators can say whose fault this is. The thread, she said, has a mind of its own. She knew uncommon things and sometimes shared them. Her dying months were hers alone, private, door shut on everyone. Pumiced cheeks and nose, a cold ear he often spoke into. He holds Rascal's hot little head between his hands. He plays his knuckles on the whippet's sharp ribs. The dog croons desolately, delightedly, at the touch. The kitchen, the morning, are best for crying. Then the teabags, the kettle, the milk. The walk upstairs, good care on the polished treads. Toe to the door, a wobble of the tray to be sure his beloved still loves him enough to allow him a few slopped tea-drops.

The second- is cranky as a bear woken in winter. The third- has knapped on his door and hallooed. He's tight-eyed, she notes, hollower in the places where middle-age bones cave in first. But he is lifted to see her, her clear, open face, and together they go to raise the fourth-. The fourth- is wound in a hotel blanket, purple fleece, and they call him a right royal fucker! They shove past into his room and spread out. The third- thinks they should be nuzzling, grunting in long-time greeting, and the second- jumps back when she tries it on him. He's not one of her dog-babies! He's paid for hair, she knows. And she's lost the pounds she needed to. Back and forth, this badinage, until the fourth- turns away to the window and shudders in the blanket. He can't put words to it, and if he tries he will drown. Poor Buster's wiped out! The third- to the rescue. Travelling for days. You're not wise! She folds him to herself, his anguish that far outmatches hers. So. Here we are, says the second-, and this place is a kip. Tell me there's more! The fourth- finds the piece of paper with a restaurant name. She loved this place, he says, something about some famous soup. And they go, and to the peace talks house and the falls and fissures and fjords. For a week they manage one another chivalrously, warming up near the end, better questions, answers that rummage more deeply for detail. The Blue Lagoon is last, where they kick one another under the milky mineral water and look for one another's spectral heads when the air gets sleety. Their father dreams of someone unsuitable who loved him years ago, whose kisses were wet and disconcerting, and the dream wakes him vexed because it wasted the time he usually spends searching for the first-. Their mother works to free a small car from a game of traffic jam she found on the phone. Rascal brings his tongue back to his tail to find the last flea, and fails.

Maenads in the Terminal

Outside the airport windows, in brown and brutal June,
little vehicles ran attendance on the tarmac. They were
dizzy as bullocks in severe afternoon heat, moving fitfully
and stopping with sickening brusqueness. I was watching
it all from the edge of a crepuscular trench that passed for
a bar-restaurant. Alchemically cool air circled my ankles,
sedulous as an old farm-cat. A massive bag came loose
from one of the trailers, fell hard, bounced dead. I jumped
at this shock to the logistics, and I'd swear the bag pulsated,
out there in the throttling hour of three o'clock EST. After
all, people sneaked creatures across borders all the time.
They drugged cubs and jammed turtles into lunch boxes.
They wanted secretions from foetuses for their eyelifts and
erections, they wanted tigers walking chained and stoned
inside their big kahuna fences. And if a creature were in
that fallen bag, would it have a chance at getting free? An
enterprising puff adder might flee for the pipes and rise a
week later in a Florida toilet. It might regard its ceramic
surrounds optimistically and wait to bite the nearest low-
hanging thing. I was departing a country where a fugitive

snake could become a celebrity. My luggage was packed tight as ten years of exile. During those years lots of people had died, and I hadn't travelled in their honour.

I had passed through security in hotshot style, lights popping and voices raised high as weapons. I wore zipless, unriveted garments, and a pad that if soaked through in an hour I was to call an emergency. Anything could happen in the latter stages of menopause. My face was more estranged each day in the mirror, steamrolled and fuzzy like one of those Renaissance painting restorations gone wrong. Beast Jesus, I'd come to address myself. Beast Jesus, what's on your docket today?

Ma'am. *Ma'am.* You're going to have to take out whatever's in your pocket.

A young woman in a toy sheriff's badge.

My pocket bulged with a mega-bottle of supplements. I rattled my flaxseed at her serene and honest face, I brandished my wild yam, ginseng, and dong quai.

See? Is that enough for you?

She flushed and apologised poignantly. It was in the nature of her generation to believe in natural healthfulness and wellbeing on a cosmic scale. All I had to do was place my herbal enhancements in the tray with shoes and bag. I did so with showy care, as if handling undischarged ordinance. She thanked me for my cooperation, and I spent my time in line recalibrating the drinks I'd have time for before boarding.

I liked what you said to Little Miss Robocop over there.

A man bellied up to the bar beside me and pistoled two fingers at the security gates.

I've all sorts of things in my mind to put to them, he said, but I always bottle out. In case I'll be taken behind the scenes for a trouncing. Under which conditions I'd probably say something even stupider.

He had the rapid-fire shyness of a Clareman and the mariner build of Tom Crean. For a time, an empty, lonely Arctic season, I used to think Tom Crean the ideal domestic partner. Away for months at a time, he was a dependable hand in the heroic age of exploration. He wore a hat fangled from the sleeve of a jumper and his arms held litters of pups. After all his Polar escapades, Tom Crean got buried in Annascaul, the anklebone of a southern county and not the white washbasin of the world. A sexy, self-effacing life well-lived.

Like what? I asked. What stupider thing?

I was waiting for my drink to be shaken and then I'd budge away to one of the dejected tables near the back.

Oh, I've lied to them before, just to get a rise. I said my wife and child weren't my wife and child and they were holding me against my will. Jesus, their faces. I had to!

I said it wasn't funny. Stupid, yes, but not funny. He said I took no prisoners.

I knew it when I saw you rattling the meds. Life's too short, isn't it, to take prisoners?

He asked if I'd take a drink.

I've a lovely one on the way, I said, shivers of ice and a pimento olive.

At the end of the bar a young waistcoat was titrating gin as neatly as a Borgia preparing a snifter. I said I had to get on my laptop a bit before the flight.

Fair enough, he said. And we might be here for a while longer. They stopped a raft of planes going out earlier because the noses were overheating. It's like the planet Jakku out there!

He waved his hands at where he thought the airport windows were. Jakku, I tell you!

Dunes and desert badlands, I said.

He granted it had been hundred and ten, more or less, and no relenting. I told him people insisted I saw more of America once they knew I was leaving it. Such an immense and varied place! Really, seriously, they counselled, you should take in more coastlines before they vanish. They had made peace with the blasted future and spoke of their landmass like a wedding buffet about to be taken away.

Have you seen the heat map of Australia, though, he said with a shudder. Continent's utterly fucked.

He cracked his knuckles and went looking for Australia on the phone.

Behold. Purple to black in the middle. Magenta round the coast. New tones for when it hits 140 or more because they ran out of oranges and reds.

He lamented that he'd never get to see the Red Centre.

I heard the indigenous dot paintings are meticulous. Beautiful, he mourned. They're supposed to hold secrets, like where water could be found.

I was moved by his ardent attention to a lost Australia, but my olive was being lanced, my glass softly wiped for overspill. I asked if he'd seen that big bag come off the luggage cart.

Was it blue? he yelped. Any chance blue, with an orange bandanna on one of the handles? Was it?

No, red, I said, a hard-shell the size of a wardrobe.

I'll sort that, he said to the bartender, who had placed the glass before me. I'll sort this lady's drink with my own.

No, I said, don't be daft. No need whatsoever.

We won't argue, he said, and patted my hand. You can get the next one if we're stuck here longer.

I left for a table with my drink and laptop bag. He chuckled. Mind the blue light doesn't give you seizures.

I set up at the back of the trench and latched onto wi-fi. I sat close to the screen in a sacral hunch. The martini gave off good sillage like an enduring perfume. The live event happened five months ago and the link to the recording was private, family and friends. I'd been married to the man for three years of our artless and indigent youth, during Dublin, throughout Cork, and/or including an aborted effort at New Zealand. I was sent the details by someone I didn't know who said she found me on social. She thought I ought to know, no matter the interstellar length of time that had passed. She was sure he would want me to know.

At different times I'd logged on to watch the recording, always tussling with the password and all the better things there were to do. I kept the password written on bits of paper, my wrist, the flyleaves of books. It was a vulgar combination of upper- and lower-case letters, not one poetic number among them. I smeared my wrist and closed the book and kept fending off the funeral. But here in this gap between one realm and another, I swelped some extra-dry off the top and pressed Play. Bits and packets slowly downloading, I raised my glass to the man at the bar. He turned and stepped forward, but I put my hand in the air. I pointed to the screen, as if it held the most urgent and confidential work in the world. His mouth pouted an acceptance and he turned back to the pond-coloured beer in his stein.

The funeral's opening moves had the cheap, jerky speed and severe light of a daytime soap. The setting was a long, blue-carpeted conference room. Before things got going, the cameraperson hissed orders to someone very nearby, and that person huffed and made staticky sounds. People straggled in and headed for the front rows. Some turned abruptly and sought back seats, like students who don't want to get asked any questions. I knew nobody. Then two young men who had his profile took the first row. Surely sons. They were massive and alien in black polyester. A young woman in a pencil skirt and pin-combed hair was tending to them. She pointed out people, whispered names in their ears. She adjusted big petals on the flowers that said FATHER. She was deft and pretty at her work, deferential to one son more than the other. I paused on them to wonder what kind of child they might make.

Two small elderly women navigated the bar tables, assessing them for cleanliness until they settled on the one next to mine.

Mind? one of them said. Mind if we do?

They looked like twins, with the same ice-white long hair and fluttery, British mannerisms.

We have a nice rosé coming our way, said the other. Though I expect it will be crudely ruddy, not the pale shades of Provence.

The bartender brought their bottle in a silver bucket. He set glasses before them and poured with the correct twist of his wrist to stop the flow.

To your good health, the first maiden said to me. To your safe travels, said the other.

The first maiden's hair was whiter, more evenly, expertly shining. The second maiden's hair had a very faint nicotine stain. She had been the less pretty one back when it must have mattered, when both of them still enjoyed the attention accorded to redheads. I nodded, raised my glass to their good fortune, and went back to the funeral.

In the row behind the sons was the woman who'd been my mother-in-law for the course of several Christmases. She was prone to theatrical rig-outs. I'd recognise the hat anywhere, a big, grey-netted confection like a beekeeper's bonnet. Every dog she'd ever owned was the size of a teacup and all of them had kidney stones. She tolerated me in a cold manner, the kind of taciturnity that got people vying for her attention. I called her the Rings of Saturn and counted down every minute survived in her orbit. Whirling rocks and debris, place of freezing death. Now she dabbed a lace-edged hanky to her face.

At the table next door, the ice-maidens had changed their seating arrangement. Now they sat shoulder to shoulder, parallel with me, and they couldn't help themselves.

It's a funeral, isn't it, dear? You're attending a funeral, poor thing. How sorry. How very sorry we are.

They pushed their glasses of rosé a few inches away, out of respect. I thanked them and insisted they didn't take it on.

Thin sawing strings struck up. One of the maidens muffled a cry, so I found the earbuds and nestled them in. Now the man from the bar was scanning for a table too. Adagio for Strings. Samuel Barber was devastating in an ancient, quarrying way. Who had picked this? The young woman, maybe. Young people often overegg already plangent situations. I wanted to tell whoever would listen a Samuel Barber story. The man had taken a wobbly table and gone to his knees, sliding a bunched paper napkin under the one perfidious leg. Driving somewhere in America, Samuel Barber turned on the radio. Adagio for Strings. Changed the station. Adagio for Strings. Another station, again Adagio, encore Adagio for Strings. JFK had been killed and Adagio was scoring the whole country's grief. Samuel Barber didn't have a clue. I loved him in the middle of his road trip, his confusion and not knowing that America's heart was shocked and broken.

Then some sect of minister in a pressed linen suit entered the screen and took the lectern. He stretched at the waist, left and right like a dancer, and cleared his throat. The camera loved his aged but lineless face and got close.

The maiden nearest me removed my right earbud and said, He's a dashing type of cleric, isn't he?

We judge and rank them, said the other. What else is there to do when you go to so many of these bloody things?

I won't keep you long, the dashing cleric said. The family has asked me to keep proceedings brief, in keeping with the deceased's wishes.

I can tell he has an unprepossessing voice, said the maiden without an earbud. He won't make it all about him. Some of them do that, you know.

I let the listening maiden stay tuned in rather than take back a sticky earbud. The other pressed close and got given the earbud every so often. They had an amiable ethics of care that made me think they were lovers, not siblings.

In the twenty minutes that followed, people stood up and sat down and did pompous things in service of the event. Someone read a very long poem, someone else sang a scripture.

I liked the person who read the poem. Seemed like a teacher. And I liked the poem too. Do not go gently into that good night. But that singer! A jackdaw. A crow.

I should think I'll go kicking and screaming. I shall be a holy living terror!

The maidens laughed like children plotting dire mischief.

The sons stayed in place throughout, their backs broad and dark and unmoving. Only when the cleric stepped out and onto the carpet did they stand and turn with a military click. They joined him at the edges of the coffin and began to push the trolley out of view.

Beautiful wood, said the first maiden, and she stroked the cheap bar table as if to conjure smooth poplar under her knotty hand. Simply. Beautiful.

The young woman in the pencil skirt faced the camera now and held her hands at half-prayer.

The Irish can be pretty when they've a mind to, said the unprettier maiden. That young actress, for example. The one who emigrated to New York.

My ex-mother-in-law was the first out of her row. A congregant offered his hand in condolence, and she swatted it away with a glove.

Gosh! That's keen, said the first maiden. I wholly admire that kind of character.

What are we watching, ladies? What's the big draw in this corner?

The man who looked less like Tom Crean by the minute rocked up before us and craned to see the screen. His ready, unreconstructed smile was grey in the laptop's light.

We are observing the rites and proceedings of death, said the first maiden. Press Pause, for goodness sake.

She tapped my hand vexedly.

Please leave us to our drinks and our colloquy, said the other, coldly.

Until now I hadn't noticed the second rosé lolling in the bucket. The maidens had been pouring their glasses with a magician's sleight. I slugged martini to put some daylight between me and the bottom of the glass. The episode was to be followed by cremation, but the camera wasn't going there. The cleric had asked everyone to keep the deceased in their prayers.

I wanted to see if this good woman would like another drink, he said, and placed his hand on my arm.

Be gone, sir, said the chillier maiden. Don't let the door hit you on the way out.

The other burst out laughing.

The door! A door, in this dive!

She calmed herself and lifted out the two empty bottles.

Apologies on behalf, she said. And ours is a Côte du Someplace. The bar tender knows. He has a marvellous name, Vercingetorix or Achilles or something like that. Thank you, my good man. You know what to ask for.

Out in the terminal people ran and rolled their way to their gates. They bickered and fumed, looked hypertense and unready. A small boy ran away from his group, throwing himself into the sprint like Philippides bringing big news to Athens. Joy to you, we've won! And then he died.

What's that? Who died? Sometimes I don't know *what* you're saying!

The man was acting like an insider, as if he and I were travelling together, or at least familiar. I hadn't known I spoke aloud. He placed a martini within my reach and slid a fresh rosé into the bucket.

Now. Where were we? Who'll fill me in?

The maidens said we were watching a funeral, though whose it was was highly dubious. They had their private theories, and they certainly had their highlights, but they deferred to me to explain. They turned their flushed faces to me like flowers to sun. Now I saw they had both been beautiful, neither one of them currying special advantage.

I said it was someone important to me at one point and for a short time.

That's awful, the man said. That's very sad entirely. And what of?

The maidens were surprised that the cleric hadn't brushed the cause of death. At the funerals they attended these days, it was commonplace to give details, or at least enough insinuative material to frighten people.

Rilke, said the maiden who had slapped me with a piano teacher's quick hand. *You must change your life.* By which he means it's not all about achieving the body beautiful, is it? There is much more to extending one's life chances than having a splendid torso.

I said I didn't know the cause of death but suspected something sudden. I had no grounds for this speculation, but it might close the case around the table.

That's the best that can be hoped, the man said. The very best of both worlds.

What both worlds, said the maiden who disliked him more violently. What are those worlds of yours that sudden death could be the best of them?

You sound like a poet, her counterpart said. You sound like a bleak little poet!

Her voice was higher now, exasperated.

I hope you'll not be so rude to the air stewards, she continued. Or our fellow passengers, for that matter.

She looked to the man and me for backing.

That one. She's a caution and a liability. How else can I put it?

Her counterpart wangled out of the seat and toed the linoleum as if it were ice. Then she began her slow, mistrustful trek to the ladies' room.

I'm losing her, the first maiden said. She shouldn't be drinking, not a drop. Not with the time she has left. But I love her too much to say no.

How very sad, I said.

And how very beautiful, the man said mournfully.

With these words he edged his chair closer to mine. Then, in an even lower tone, he said, *The weight of the world is love*. I heard it one time and I've never forgotten.

His skill with vocal registers was chilling.

For a long and wordless time, we sat waiting for the other maiden to return. Flights were announced for the last time, doors were about to close. Names were called, struggles in the pronunciation of some, then called for the very last time. The maiden at the table stood shakily to her feet, but only because the other maiden was finally wayfaring back from the loo. Her eyes were luminous and tearful, as if she had learned something astounding and catastrophic during her dank time in the ladies'.

Now, she said to the man. When do we get to rend *you* limb from limb?

My dear, my dear, said the maiden in charge. What have I told you, what have I asked you? Remember the kindness of strangers.

No, you old torch, said the other. You won't silence me that easily.

When I heard some scratchy version of my name across the tannoy, I drained the glass and shut the laptop. I excused myself to forge a path past the tables and chairs. I stopped to pluck lycra from behind my knees, where leggings tend to bunch in the course of a day.

You missed a spot, my dove.

The second maiden, narrow-eyed and satisfied as a detective.

It's already a sticky old business, flying overseas. Give yourself the best chance, won't you? Here. Shall I loosen the problem for you?

She advanced a few steps to help with my dishevelment. I plucked between my cheeks.

Dear, she said. You've only gotten yourself stuck at the front. Where it always looks worse, don't you think? Especially at your station in life.

The other maiden sat down heavily, as if never to rise again.

Yes, she said, appeasing and broken in spirit. Yes, let's tear this man into pieces.

Her voice was emollient as a midnight radio presenter of the world's greatest love songs. If she continued speaking, I was in danger of staying to join the conniption.

After all, she went on, he did get us quite, quite drunk. We're no longer compos mentis and responsible for our actions.

The other maiden smiled ravenously and shivered in delight.

Let's! It's very apropos! Let's!

The man remained stationed. His shoulders were dropped now, as if waiting for the first to fall in a rain of blows. There was a time when the man I was married to went looking in the car seat crevices for coins. He came back to the flat round-shouldered and savage with self-hatred.

I got to the bar and left my card. I told the bartender to tot it all up, whatever might be needed at the back table from here to the end of time. Behind me the maidens had stopped shouting at each other and threatening Tom Crean with dismemberment. Now their voices came dancing after me, importuning me to come back and join their cause. I picked up speed in the rapids of Terminal B. Blood coursed down from my core, and a gust of weakness nearly capsized me. All I had to do was make it to the door and get out of this neck of the bloodying woods.

In the Inn District

It was still dim, even at ten in the thinning morning. Twenty years ago I was one of hundreds of recruits. A skinnymalink in 60 denier and big surplus boots, I enlisted in Galway City. What flats there were were as scarce as Soviet bread, and the queues to rent them were ruthless. It was the age of tuna from the tin and cider from the tap. Everyone ballooned in winter and got famished by May. Decimation meant the death of every tenth person, and maybe that happened too. Mothers didn't know us off the buses, and fathers asked no questions.

Hans Castorp said the flatlands was the place he left behind to go to the Magic Mountain. One month after being conferred with the knowledge of all of German literature, or as much as could be gleaned in four years of late-afternoon lectures at a university that hadn't given flesh to funding frameworks, I said goodbye. I forsook the small bars with their nooks and snugs, the bladderwrack and the trawlers. It was the summer of the pine marten scandal, a vendor in the arty Saturday market selling the tree cat's secretions as love drugs. It was a city where new-fangled things got contagious then miserable. I was surprised to get out in one piece and unpoisoned.

In London I lived in shabby isolation in a half-transfigured garage. The windows were higher than I could reach to see. In winter the landlady gave me a bedspread. She was an anxious Ealing creature, sphinxlike in her wrinkles, and she smoked in bed. She was afraid she'd set herself, the room, the house ablaze.

But I can't give up my most loyal and beloveds, she said, tapping two Windsor Blues on the table.

She had read unsolved-crime-mysteries where an ashen pair of slippers was the last thing left. Combustion, she said, was a terrible way to go.

Take it! she ordered, and pushed yellow chenille on me. The bedspread undulated eerily, an enchanted fleece shorn from the last of a species. In a deadly house fire, my garage would be the last bit standing and still I wouldn't see a thing, only scudding clouds and a thousand-volt yard light that searched like a prison break.

In America I would learn the word *afire*, which was a better, finer word for the suddenness of women in flames.

If the world were ending in a month. Okay? Let's say a month. Not six, not a year. You might not have that long. A month focuses things. So, a month. And say you had the resources to travel unlimitedly. Where would you want to go?

Someone got this question going at our supper club, supper clubs being what happen when you turn the gate for forty in a country not of your making. I'd been teaching English to the children of German auto-makers in a series of southern United States states. I advanced around the map like a heat rash, following the work where it was. The auto-makers wanted a scholarly register and paid well for the labour.

One time I told Mercedes kids if they didn't pay attention I'd teach them *The Sorrows of Young Werther*. When they heard it took Werther half a day to die after shooting himself in the head, they were transported.

Please! Please, Miss!

I said it would be much too much for their tender hearts, and anyway I'd be fired.

They didn't care if I got fired as long as they heard about Werther.

We negotiated an agreement to build slowly to Werther, to earn him by moving through alienation, isolation, and *Das Intimleben des Adrian Mole*. The children of German auto-makers loved that sebaceous, whiny twerp.

So. Come on now. The supper club. Where would you all go for your month?

This was before people came to acknowledge the pain and dying of the world, and answers involved a predictable ravening. Suckling pigs cooked beneath banana leaves, coral reefs in the southwest Pacific. Bali.

David Bowie's ashes had been scattered there. Someone said she still burst into tears at the mention of him, in spite of the time that had passed.

I just can't, she said. I can't believe he's not in this world anymore.

He never was, someone advised. He was always only ever visiting. Goodbye, spaceboy.

The Galapagos. Paris in spring. Yurts that opened onto beach, and plein air showers.

Someone said that everyone likes the idea of showering outdoors.

And then you do it. And you can't figure out how to look like the kind of healthy, sexed-up person who showers outdoors. And you forget the fucking towel.

They howled. Someone else was ashamed of not having hiked the Appalachian Trail. She knew it took six months at a good clip.

I felt an old twinge, the same needle that tickled me in the wretched London season, and then on the Upper East Side when I pushed cranky lawyers' crankier children in colossal strollers. It had taken a while to locate me in the southern states, heat lightning and visa disasters spinning it off course. Now that needle found all my rolling veins, and the bruises would be callous and black.

Everybody thinks they're just testing things out, my older cousin in New Zealand once said. Until they're not, because the ground has crumbled behind them, because some brigand cut the rope bridge, because, as the book said, you can't go home again.

She was an eloquent alcoholic, unattached. The kind of wedding guest everyone loved to watch swing their children around the dance floor but who nobody thought would make a good mother. Later she would fail to sing 'Carrickfergus' and beg for a chance at 'The Town I Loved So Well'.

I'm nowhere and nothing and can't hold a fucking note, she wept.

Consoling her was hazardous work, involving pints of water and anterooms to exert her unseemliness and grief. I held her by the shoulders like she was a bloodied boxer and I sending her to the ring to get killed again.

She marshalled herself to try Morrissey. She made a good show of 'Everyday is Like Sunday'.

She always left for New Zealand next day.

I told them Galway. That's where I would fetch up for the month.

Ireland! Someone had been to Ireland. She couldn't understand why menus all over the country said 'mixed veg'.

Like they don't want to say what the vegetables are. Because the knowledge would be too much.

The supper club said they'd scuttle all their ships and itineraries, their exotic islands where rare animals walked up to befriend you, and join me in Galway instead.

Hire a bus, go region by region. So. Much. Fun!

The man who devoted his life to Thomas Bernhard looked round the supper club and said we were crazy. Ireland was low, very low on his list. Its best writers were beermats by now, the whole place PTSD'd from the Church.

He had taught a long time at a university and resigned because Thomas Bernhard meant nothing to the narcissistic stresses of Generation Z. We dallied round one another for a time, extracurricular to the supper club. Open mics with unwashed, jilted poets, flat whites and pastries in the park. There were surreptitious promises of astonishing sex and long international films. *The Mysteries of Lisbon* and *Sátántangó*.

He was trying to turn a Bernhard book into a podcast and wanted me to rehearse. He would play the main character, I his disabled wife. I sat for hours on a cushionless chair while he spoke one sentence into my ear.

In the inn district it is still dim.

I told him it was a terrible idea for a podcast. People listened for talk, variety, liveliness. Human interest and the spice of life.

What if I told you he killed her? he said. Do you think they'd all listen then?

I agreed that many podcasts hinged on a dead body and threatened to stop seeing him.

You're declining me with full intentionality, he mourned. You're choosing not to persevere with this journey.

He added he'd always thought I had a paltry imagination, for literature and language, liquors and wines, liquors needing courage, wine a finer palate. Travel, even, and pets.

Everyone says Labrador, *everyone*. The golden friendliness. Please.

When I told the supper club I was sinking my money into a foreclosed guesthouse in Galway, they couldn't compute. Where again? Near a greyhound track? Their own dreams of magical places had died during winter. Now it was all about getting kids into college. It was rankings, athletics and meal plans. Everyone was tight on money.

We had been kind to one another for a time, for years. We scrupulously brought one another to appointments, to follow-ups when the results were dubious. They wanted to but didn't take me out to say goodbye.

Mind how you go, said Thomas Bernhard. Make sure there's no MSG in the mixed veg.

*

There was a pall from coal smoke.

Would you believe it, said the woman who walked off the bus before me. Some people are gone back to bituminous. Renegades!

She said she used to be a college professor and before that an activist. When I looked more closely, she might have been a suffragette, one hundred and ten years old.

I think the smoky coal crowd like being part of the cause of the end of the world. This is the west of Ireland. The liminal edge. They think the worst to happen will happen here last.

We walked companionably on the greasy paving stones.

I'm from down in Clare, the woman said. We see things very clearly. It's just a painful curse. Worse times, though, it comes on as a migraine. A bastard behind the eyes, like your man Withnail!

She stopped at the red door of a dark bar.

I don't know if they're doing sandwiches with the soup today. Nor if the sandwich will be made with a roof rat or flakes of foot fungus. But it's worth a try, in the unceasing hope for human decency. Goodbye to you and enjoy your stay!

She was a tonic welcome back to daftness. I should have told her I was here for the duration.

I gained the hill and the morning lifted.

Thomas Bernhard breathed in my ear. I stood at the midpoint of a street of guesthouses. Vacancies all the way, and every second name something mystical, Arthurian.

Mine had never had a name, the agent said. It changed hands several times, and nobody made a go of it as a business. The agent blamed the parsimony of the sharing economy.

Shameless carry-on! Unprofessionals. Renting out a utility room and calling it a Room for the Kids. And people stupid enough to pay the night's money.

I didn't want to make a go of it either. I wanted rooms where people might come to gather without my entertaining them. William James smoked a pipe in the library while his wife did social reproduction in the drawing room. I'd come back to this city, this country, to dock, but I'd leave for upstairs when the ground floor turned into the Walls of Limerick.

We all, said Thomas Bernhard, we all crave return to the mother country's bosom.

But when asked, he wouldn't tell where he was from. He sounded Anglo-Australian. One of the supper club said, don't believe it for a second. He's the quintessence of self-invention. That asshole is from the Florida mangroves!

My mother and father lived in an outpost of deepest Cork. Tradition had it that I landed with them each Christmas, and again for two weeks in summer. Everything went kindly and courteously, in the way of familiar strangers. We tried to make the old places new. Beach towns and the bars of hotels. Bingo, even, for silly, screaming laughs, though the bawdy ways of calling numbers had been cleaned up.

You can't say two fat ladies anymore, my mother said. Nor legs-eleven. It's misogynistic. Or do I mean sexist? Which is the worse one? Is it? Really! Anyway. You know what I mean. You just can't say the old things anymore.

Describe your parents, Thomas Bernhard had commanded,

as though my answer would determine our forging a life together.

Soft, gentle creatures, I said, after a long time. And persistent all the same.

He said they sounded like snow. I had no gift for depiction, he said, and in that I failed the saints and scholars.

His own were two people he should put in pots, he said.

Like the play. Surely you know Beckett. Mine, they'd want the pot fitted with all the comforts. Electric blankets and Chivas Regal. And USB to charge the phones.

Mine were bamboozled about the B&B.

We don't entirely understand, my mother said. We don't understand at all. After all this time, Galway?

But they supposed I'd make a go of the place because in their estimation I was old enough and had always been independent. They put a hefty amount to the deposit because they said we would all make the money back.

All the tourists in summer. Mighty! And the race crowd. And you can lodge students the rest of the year.

Thomas Bernhard said it was their insurance.

This is how they lure you. Home is so sad. It stays as it was left, shaped to the comfort of the last to go, as if to win them back. They've been reading Philip Larkin.

I said it should be nothing to him. We hadn't bothered one another for months.

I know, he said. It's just I see the bigger picture and have no choice but to inform you. Now go back to that second image of the kitchen. Heathenly fuck.

A guesthouse? More like a transport to Australia.

If this was what the supper club meant by abuse, the

nonchalant knowing better and predicting worse, then he was a mastermind.

In any case the place was rock-bottom because the yard for parking was the size of a sock. And the lights and the noise from the greyhound track. And the last owners' mortgage calamity. Their fleeing. Then burst pipes, a hole in the roof, starlings and pigeons and bats.

Poor things, said my mother, in the abstracted tone she had for other people's distant disasters. It's hard to get going these days.

She said I'd always had romantic stirrings for derelict houses.

What I had were colours to paint and plans for distressing the furniture.

The first dog showed up when the builder finally, rancorously, finished his work.

He's taking too long, my father railed. He's taking the piss entirely! Tell him you know what's what.

I did, but the builder was unmoved.

You have to see things my way, the builder said. I do one bit of your job and let it settle, and I move onto my other job, and let that settle, and so on and so forth. And then I come back round to you. Capiche?

A Connemara racketeer, he pinched his dark eyes to unfathomability.

Just when you thought you were out, I drag you back in, is it?

My voice grappled for know-how and menace.

Ah, now. There's no need for that, Miss.

My mother said I shouldn't have been making tea and cutting sandwiches for him.

I bet you did triangles, too. That might be polite in America, but you can't do it here. Not anymore. You'll never see the end of them.

The builder left me a bill I couldn't decipher, every line item a brand-name or compound verb. Bostik and Superquilt. Tear-out, take-down, the argot of gangsters. I sat against a sanded wall and drank half a bottle of dreadful red. The sulfites and tannins were breakdancing in my chest when the greyhound walking back and forth outside the sliding door stopped and became real. It looked at me mournfully and swung away running.

Come back, I called out. I love you!

In the inn district the evening air was dense and damp. If it hadn't been for paint fumes I would have felt heavy-hearted, utterly mistaken. I had fifteen job applications travelling the SMTP highway. Their embellishments might make a better, finer person blush, but this was the age of self-peddling. You had to talk a thing up, then up.

My cousin in New Zealand would have a mystical or caustic read on the situation. In a hushed moment at a christening, she told a scattering of us she had done unguarded, contaminating things for money. The dark mystery made her our hero. She left for New Zealand next morning.

When Leonard Cohen died my mother renamed the cat Ladies' Man. When the cat went under the wheels of a tractor, my father called it Death of a Ladies' Man.

Because I was going to turn into one or other of them

anyway, I called the greyhound David Bowie, and waited and waited for him to come back.

You know he's a serial abuser of women? We think you should know, so we're telling you.

A small splinter group from the supper club had taken me for coffee to talk.

They'd known Thomas Bernhard for years, had borne him because he'd never tried to cull from their number.

But you. Of course he's trying it. You're. Young.

I waited and hoped for *and lovely*. Instead they talked about California, where technocrats were paying tens of thousands for the blood plasma of younger people.

They say it makes them feel great! See what we're saying?

Thomas Bernhard had bitten me in the stupidest, most bloodless place, my elbow. It hurt because it crunched. I listened to their tracts on a man they'd known but not known for years.

I mean, he can be very charming. He knows all the craft beers, and never brings a dud. And he never overstays his welcome. Like someone else we know.

They moved on to lamenting the disgraced football coach who left his house only to come to the supper club.

Sometimes. Okay, sometimes, I'll say it, sometimes I get the sense he hasn't showered since the last time. Is that awful of me?

We agreed it was, but it wasn't wide of the mark. But he always said the funniest thing on any given evening. And his crime had been embezzlement, not cameras and hot tubs. Thus he was forgiven. And Thomas Bernhard forgotten. True, it had been hours in that chair, him circling, trying different tones to say that one boneless sentence. No bathroom break, a urinary infection one week on. The doctor asked if there was anything else she needed to know. The elbow, the foot, the wrist. Had I been worried at by a dog?

I told her I hadn't heard the phrase since childhood. A television ad to keep your dogs from killing sheep by night. A cartoon dog ambled out from a house and joined a pack of marauders. They flung themselves into the fields and ripped the bellies of sheep. A lamb nudged its fallen mother, the dog returned to the fireside. At school we enacted the ad. Anyone who got to play the main dog sat back by its owner, with knowing flames in its eyes.

The first dog returned, with a second dog in tow. When they recruited a third they moved in. I was in no position not to yield.

Fine, I said. Let me show you to your rooms. Thank you for booking directly with us.

The fawn hound took the room with the shared blue bathroom, the white one got a sweeping view over the shallow lough. The black hound, my first visitant, took the room with the connecting door to mine. He got bay window, cushions, and a painting by the painter whose name I could never remember, but whose gentle Disney tints and Christmas cottages made me sicken for American years I hadn't had in northeastern places I'd never been.

I trained the hounds to defecate collectively. I shoveled weekly to the back corner of the back lawn. The tumulus stank until it dried out, and nobody came to track my dogs down.

I was there fixing up, painting over, walking dogs for a month before my mother and father showed up, each with a rolling suitcase. I hoped they'd brought wine but they hadn't.

Just the weekend, my mother said. The luggage was on special offer and it's great for not balling up clothes!

They'd left space for shopping to bring back to Cork. My father said there wasn't a lazier name for a commercial district than Shop Street. It was so much worse than Main Street.

The further down you go! At least you got the old joke from that one.

I gave them the vacant room, the en-suite painted Cream of Furze above the wainscoting and Enlightenment below. It took them fully half a day to run into David Bowie, then Heine and Hesse, who by then were inseparable and slept in a figure of eight.

Oh Jesus, they cried! Dogs! Dogs in the house? They'll destroy the place!

I showed them everywhere. No hair, no smell, no trace of a creature at all.

Hounds leave a light mark, I told them. They might as well be wearing slippers and hazmat, that's how clean they are.

They grudged a dog-walk by the lough. My father tried to remember a Van Morrison album.

You know the one. The one where Van and his missus. They're walking greyhounds, I'd swear it.

My mother tried to remember Van's missus's name.

A model. Beyond belief, a woman so good-looking, giving him a look. But you never can tell when it comes to love. They're not still married. Are they?

My father looked out over the lough, said you could never call it a lake, not in a million. Too scrubby round the edges.

Michelle Rocca, I said.

My mother praised my power of recall, said I always remembered inconsequential things.

Michelle Rocca is important, my father contended. She took up with the most significant singer-songwriter of the twentieth century.

David Bowie hauled on the leash, drawn by a figment twitching in the bushes. Heine and Hesse sprang the other way, away from arrant nonsense. I thought I saw the ancient suffragette on the footpath by the railway line, but at this wet and windblown distance I couldn't be sure.

When my parents went shopping they got useful plastic items. Pump-action soap dispensers. Tall boxes with holes in the lids, for pouring breakfast cereals. They said no guesthouse could be without them, and reminded me to get at least one gluten-free option. They got bigger boxes still for the greyhounds' foodstuffs. Fleece blankets and a tall stand for bowls.

Think about it, my father said. Bowls on the floor, and it's a giraffe reaching down for a daisy. Very bad for digestion, impossible.

Their efforts were generous and exact. I'd never have thought of so many receptacles.

You could, my mother suggested, market this place as dog-friendly. What other guesthouse along here does that? None, I'd venture. There's any amount of biddies and crackpots out there who want to bring Rover on hols!

We parted on good terms and sandwiches packed for their train. There was talk of my going their way for Easter, their coming mine for the races. They might fit a shed with old carpet.

For the hounds! my father said.

My mother took my hand in hers. She said I looked better and fuller than when we used to FaceTime.

If I wasn't looking straight at those dogs inside the window, she said, I'd say they were my imagination.

On one of those FaceTimes Thomas Bernhard said he'd stay out of sight and make no sound. I used earphones to guard the jolly, abrasive voices of my parents.

My father said he had an awful notion there was a control freak nearby, telling me what to say.

I've seen it in films. Mainly American.

He always kept a bead drawn on the depravity of the US. I came away blinking from the screen, tight on the cheekbones from performing ease and serenity.

I want to soundproof you from those people, Thomas Bernhard said, moving to me with hands gasping for air. Those horrible, earsplitting people. How did you ever survive, to get away, to me, to try this thing we're about?

We went to the cork-tiled room. The chair was pulled out from the table, the cushion removed. He switched on the recorder and dictated date and time.

The hounds might well be your imagination, I told my

mother. But it would take some powerful extra thinking to project them into *his* head.

My father smiled, swept up in the thought experiment. You'd collapse from the psychic effort, I told her.

I've seen something like that, said my father. Heads imploding in a sci-fi film. Someone trying to think someone else's thoughts. The two of them went kaput.

In the window for all to witness, Heine was kissing Hesse. David Bowie stood to one side, aloof, as all strays and vagabonds must do.

Bus Shelter

You're yellow bus, the man inside glass said to Inghean. Low-voiced and pale, he had been growing for years in poor light. Cold air swarmed the airport hall and battled the despotic old heat pushing through a few hatches and holes. There were men in glass hutches all down the hall. One of them tugged and poked his ear like it was air-locked from swimming. He was the youngest of the early morning abettors, and he put the same finger to work in his nose. Inghean moved closer to hear the man she was allocated. When he spoke his glass steamed up in ghostly piebald patches. He was at home in this wheelhouse, with faith in himself and his collar and cufflinks. He was around the same age as her brother, who would never work inside glass unless the glass were architecturally beautiful or he was consuming the coastal hotel light he sought in countries on the brink of financial collapse.

Her brother lived in a north-facing house on the Vico Road described one time by design pages as a spacecraft copulating with a hill. *Here, in a hidden bower on the South Dublin coast*, the article began, *we find a conundrum of money and poor taste.* It ended with praise for the house's old cabbage palms, *planted as long ago as the War of Independence.* She had loved that column. She pinned it on the board above her desk with other snippets that made her laugh at different times in her life. She put her brother's spacecraft beside *New Yorker* cartoons of dogs disparaging their hapless owners and quotes from poets that once seemed profoundly stirring but which she found later had better, more enduring words nearby.

A small sign on the glass said, No use of mobile phones in this area, and hers was buzzing in her pocket, probably her brother, wondering how far along the morning she was. He would be in his brig, standing on Travertine tiles and watching coffee ooze its dark oil from a sleek machine. The last time she stood inside his windows she said to him, *For here there is no place that does not see you.* He said nobody saw him, not a soul. In fact, she would be surprised at the amount of privacy he enjoyed from one season to the next.

Because I paid enough for it, he said, flicking a mote from the glass.

That's Rilke, she said.

That's who?

Since then the recluses who had been his neighbours had moved to other hills, bought a house in Los Angeles that used to belong to a famous German writer. The paparazzo who skulked in their hedges, a fat little fellow always dropped off by a taxi, was gone too. Her brother told her all this on a phone call, making rounds through his house's acoustics, pacing from louder rooms to the dulling snugness of the laundry nook. Her brother missed the paparazzo more than the neighbours because, her brother said, he was a hustler. He went through recycling like a fox turning over a hen-house.

That's a nice scarf, said the man in the hutch. A nice bright colour at this glum hour.

He turned to his computer, where the field had brightened to receive her details. She slid her passport through.

I wouldn't know you there, he said, and looked up and down and up. Then he flushed because this might be a faux pas, something she would report him for. He mended the situation by saying there was only a year left on the passport.

Anyway. Short hair or long, you're grand. And you're yellow bus. Mind you heard that. Do you have someone meeting you on the other end?

She said she had a brother. Who might not recognise her, or she him. It had been a while.

In their fifties she and her brother knew one another faintly. When she moved to America in her mid-twenties their mother wept for him losing a sister. He said not to worry, he wouldn't notice Inghean was gone. He was always busy, going in at the bottom and selling off high. Neither had spouses or children, though he came closer more often. He almost succeeded in the year he wore indigo shirts and black ties and fell in love with a model from Malta. He even shaved his head shiny, like the Greek ex-minister for economics, he explained, but he didn't have the fineness of that brainy man's skull. He visited her in America every three years, preferring the city with brownstones and boulevards to the earlier small town where she made a pittance and shared a house. He always treated her to one fine dinner at the end of his stay, choosing wine from the exorbitant reds and insisting they try all the desserts.

The younger man two hutches away was rapping at his glass and glaring at her hutch.

That's the boss man, hers said. A pup. So. Yellow bus. Yellow. There's one every half hour for the next three hours, then nothing until the late afternoon. Got it?

She had, as clearly as she had followed green arrows to get this far and stopped on red lines.

Got it, she said. Yellow bus.

He looked out at her more carefully now.

Where did you get a name like that?

She told him her father had loved the old saints, the ones no one mentioned anymore.

Nobody mentions *any* saints anymore, he said. How do you pronounce it?

The 'g' is hard, she told him, and the rest he could probably manage.

She heard a murmur gathering behind her in the line and felt the weight of undue time and attention she got from this man who all day long told people to come through or wait over there. There was a long, low bench against the furthest wall, and from there people were summoned through a door so flush with the wall that it opened shallowly, like the trapping wing of a stealthy creature.

Right, he said. Sorted, then. Yellow bus. If you go at a good clip you'll make the next one and you won't have to wait in the rain.

She thanked him and took her passport back. It was warm and pliant from his hand.

Yellow. And don't take blue. Blue will only delay things for you. You, my lady—he motioned for her ticket one more time and pinched his glasses close to his eyes—you are entitled to yellow.

He curled his finger to draw her closer to the mouthpiece. She brought her ear there slowly, as though the brushed metal might emit a very dirty joke.

Let me tell you, love, he said. A few dimbos got on a blue last month, and now they're all over the newspapers, and they're crying on the radio.

He wheeled back in the tall chair.

There isn't a politician, not one, who'll get involved! Reporters are going all the way to Galway to cover their story.

She asked to be reminded if yellow went all the way to Galway too.

No, he said. God, no. Yellow is the midlands. They have the whole set-up there and you'll be sorted out. State of the art, I'm told.

He moved forward again.

Alright. Off you go, Inghean. Am I still saying it right? Good. And good luck to you.

The waist-high flaps let her past and she trundled her case at an angle to ease off the stripped, loud wheel. A few more halls and doors, and there were the buses nose-to-tail. She stood in line for yellow and watched people with children climb the steps of blue, reaching and lifting and making the small bodies as manageable as packages. A message from her brother said let him know when she needed to be picked up. He was busy, mind you, so factor that into the equation. A driver tumbled like a clown from a yellow bus, wiped his eyes and smiled enormously. It was time for his act to commence. He opened the belly of the bus and offered to sling in the bags.

The bus held one other passenger, a sexless figure sleeping deep in a hood with an insect buzz of music coming from the depths. The driver twisted the bus onto the road, wheeling hand over hand the way farmers used to do with tractors to get them between tight gate posts. The hooded figure twitched and the music got louder. A cicada worked its tymbals to frighten birds away, young people heard higher hertzes and survived. The driver braked at a roundabout and tore smoke from the road.

I love the Georgians, the driver said, jerking his thumb at red brick buildings stuck together the length of an entire street. Love. Those. Georgians. High ceilings and orange slice windows over the doors. Have you heard of the Georgians? They knew what was what.

His eyes flashed inquiry at her in the mirror. She nodded at him and looked away to the window. They flowed onto the motorway and he went quiet for an hour. Gorse and furze, flatlands and bog. The centre of the country was an open, charred wound.

You wouldn't believe the things that surface in bogs in this country.

He was back on, rolling his shoulders to soften the muscles, warming to his subject.

Nasty murders and sacrifices in the Bronze Age. Sacrifices, mark you. It was worse than *Game of Thrones*, I'd say.

She said she did know. She had read the poems and seen the photos, the twisted, gristly limbs. Perfect fingernails that looked like they'd done a day's weeding, no more.

Out there, she said, in the old man-killing parishes, I will feel lost, unhappy, and at home. Seamus Heaney.

Pardon me, he said. I didn't think you were from this country. But now I hear it. And you know your stuff, well done.

The hooded figure remained still and self-enclosed as a rock, and the driver started humming. His voice was high and weird like a theremin. She looked away so as not to catch him in the mirror. A sign had five or six locations for exiting the motorway, all three kilometres away. Car sales and furniture flocked past the window, then stands of houses with red algae stains running down their walls. Then a small park and a bar called The Hucklebuck. A premises lit like an undersea grotto offered cool sculpting of fat from one's body. Then the open road again, and soon a smaller, gravel road lined with sloe bushes and hedgerows.

The driver made a big production of arrival.

Ladies and gentlemen, he proclaimed. Persons awake and asleep. We will be dismounting at the front left of this vehicle, where I will place a step for your safety and comfort.

The hooded figure rose and drew the cowl away. He looked as fresh as if he had slept in an Alpine field in summer.

I'm sure you have someone to collect you when you're finished here, the driver said. But if there's some mistake, you can try to get back the same way with me again.

He said his bus left once a week and always at midday. Wait, wait, wait the.

The young man was swiping his phone and excitedly tapping.

This isn't where I'm going. I'm supposed to be. Here.

The driver looked at the screen.

You're right, he said. That's not here. That's away in Mayo. Why didn't you take blue?

The young man held the phone to his chest with both hands and breathed hard through his nose.

Settle yourself. This happens, the driver said. Jet lag and people wandering out in the darkness. I'll take you back on this yellow, back to the beginning, and from there you'll get blue. Although it might be tomorrow.

He turned his dials on Inghean.

You? Were you meant to be on yellow?

He had a mild truculence now. She assured him a red bus picked up at this junction. He said he hadn't dealt with red but knew it was in the system.

When the footstool was taken up into the bus, and the bus wheels popped their last bit of gravel, there was nothing for her but a bench and a shelter. The bench was narrow and inclined downwards so she had to partly squat and clench her knees up and under. The cloudy Perspex siding was etched with profanities. There were penises, too, and skulls and bombs and two people's names in capital letters. Seán hearting Sheila forever. Inghean traced the names until the crosshatching got hazy and snarled.

She drowsed a few minutes in the pulsing silence of

the countryside. Alone and stout-hearted in an unknown corner, she didn't know what counties she abutted. A spell of drizzle finished in an hour and left the air steaming. She waited for red.

So, her brother said on their last call before she booked the flight, I'll ask you one more time. Why?

He was nonplussed and suspicious. Why the big move back, when the economy was in the tank? When there were limits and quotas on who got back in and who could stay? And why, of all the whys, at her age?

Anyone who left a long time ago, he said, anyone who pinned their colours to another mast is under review. Subject to.

Subject to what, she asked?

No one knows, he said.

Last year she saw a woman in a newspaper asked about her return. Caught shy in Arrivals, she said she had lived a long time away. *I hate to tell you*, the woman answered, *thirty-five years*, as if her time away was a terrible secret, a long-running infidelity during which both parties grew old and hopeless about their prospects of being together.

Her brother said someone he went to school with shut up a financial brokerage on a small, beautiful island and divorced a woman and left a child.

That's how much he wanted back. And now he's in some holding place off the west coast. Pending. No one knows. But you'll be fine. You're on the fast track. They'll pop you through a few questions and let you go.

He told her not to be too professional, though, not highbrow.

They'll think you're taking the piss.

When the bus drew up by her shelter, it was tall and white and red and old, with a scuffed red setter emblazoned on its side. She didn't want to leave her bench and the history of love engraved all around her. The bus sighed and steamed and its door slid aside, delivering a smartly dressed woman and man. Each held a little computer tablet.

Stay where you are, the woman said. No need to move.

The door sealed behind them and the bus went gingerly over the gravel. Then the man spoke.

Because our facility is currently experiencing flooding from burst pipes during the recent unexpected freeze and sudden thaw, we will conduct your interviews here at this facility.

He was punctilious and thin, with a far western burr in his voice.

We tend to begin with lone travellers, said the woman with the tablet. So we'll start with you.

One of them wore a sweet, yeasty scent.

The woman motioned for Inghean's permission to sit down. The obstinate bench posed her no problems, and she began pecking at her screen with long white nails. The man walked away and pecked at a distance.

Inghean agreed that yes, that was she. Yes, those were the various digits and addresses according with her life. The preliminary stuff passed easily enough. How long she had lived away, how often she returned, nature and duration of former employment, existence of spouses and children.

None? The woman looked up for the first time. Oh, I see.

Not to worry. It's not for everyone, is it?

The woman's shoulders were looser now and her gaze more conversational.

I suppose it's easier to move about the world. I've had women tell me that. Have you found it so?

Inghean said yes, to a certain extent.

She had moved about holiday cities alone and come back to a dank apartment, the kitchen fruity from bins she had forgotten to take out. She had moved around the apartments of dinner parties where it became clear at a certain time of night that she was there on offer to some single person or other. She had moved to standing and weeping at the end of ballet and theatre performances and was often the first to reach the front doors to the street.

Any pets? the woman asked. No, let me re-order that. Any contact with farm animals in the past six months? Then any pets?

No contact, Inghean said. And yes.

She had sublet the remaining months on her apartment and her last dilemma had been The Laird. She wanted her sheltie documented on the woman's officious little device, the blue-coated creature left behind in his ninth year. He had three or so years left in the company of the gay couple she finally found. Those keen, kind men had a mountain climate in summer and no smaller pets for the chase. On the bus shelter bench, beside this woman taking account, she flushed with longing for The Laird.

She was asked to spell her name, and a second time, as though it were a password to be tested for correctness. She was asked about remaining money in banks, creditors, association memberships, vaccinations, involvement in class action suits.

The man was coming back now.

Did you ask her about friends, foes, trolling? Those are my favourites to maggot out of people, and for no reason at all!

His voice was travelling, ranging across a plane of accents and landing on a clipped British note.

Last week I canned an application because someone had bad blood with a boyfriend. What can I say? I had a low quota to make and this one tulip came along with trouble in the bag.

He drew a chocolate bar from his pocket and unpeeled the golden wrapper in long, tinselly strips. He waved it at the woman—want some?—then half-heartedly at Inghean.

I can't tell you how many people on my list get misty-eyed for crappy chocolate like this. And the vinegar crisps of their youth. Nostalgia runs something fierce through my forty-somethings. A man cried the other day because his mother used to send him chocolate in New York in the height of summer and it arrived melted through the envelope and destroyed the inside of those nice-looking boxes with little brass doors you see on television.

He sat by Inghean and turned to her with something like affection.

Did you have one of those mailboxes?

She said yes, for a time. And then another, outside a front door, that froze shut in winter. She had to bring a hot kettle down and fling the contents at the metal.

Right, he said. Without getting scalded. Fair play. Now,

if my colleague has completed her preliminary work, then you and I will move on to the second stage.

His colleague shut her tablet and walked around the shelter. She pored over the inscriptions like the first person who went into a pyramid with a lamp. The air was filling with a sour pollen Inghean couldn't place, a building, dizzying stink. When had she last been on her feet? But when she tried to stand up the man directed her back down. She thought she heard the slouching sound of a bus.

She said her jet-lag was kicking in. She should be calling her brother soon to collect her.

Not for a while, he said. We have more to discuss.

He worked at lumps of chocolate inside his cheeks as he spoke.

What does this brother of yours do for a living and will he be supporting you while you wait the requisite year before seeking employment?

She told the man her brother was good enough to give her space and time to set up.

Is he indeed? And then what? What's out there for you?

She said she might resume teaching.

You might? he said. At your age?

Maybe at a private school.

May. Be. I don't see a lot of jobs like that left going. My sister's been trying to break in for years. She'd love a private school job. Miss Brodie. Who wouldn't!

The sun was high and white now. She shaded her eyes with a faltering hand. A horse whickered beyond the high hedgerow. She had always loved that sound, lassitude and forbearance in one long, wet soughing off of the world.

The woman ducked her head round from the back of the shelter and raised her hand at her colleague, fingers spread wide. She mouthed a word.

Yes! Thank you, he said. What, he turned to Inghean, is your five-year-plan? We can't process any application that doesn't have a five-year-plan.

He wasn't taking notes. Inghean wasn't even sure he had a tablet anymore. Maybe the woman was recording things.

Oh. Oh, surely not, the woman gasped.

She pointed to a high corner of the Perspex, to some image hiding up there.

Surely not, the woman went on, her head tilted towards her shoulder.

Go on, the man said. The next five years. Where do you see yourself?

Significant ties, her brother had said. Give them the haggard orchard and the field and the house.

He and she had grown up in a house that came to a standstill in her name. Their parents gone, the fields waist-high until a steadfast neighbour brought out his mower. She had leased it for years from afar, first to farmers who left the house mouldering because they wanted only the land, then to a family who let the chimney go on fire. She nearly sold it last year because her brother said she was cursed with trying to manage it. She had travelled back for the week of the sale.

It's the right thing to do, he said then. There's no emotional attachment remaining. How could there be, so old and damp? Radon menacing the floor.

He would never get over Inghean being left the house. He would grouse about it privately, by night, with a drink, looking out on the dark forms of his cabbage palms. The downcast week of the auction was like one long, poorly lit day, and by the end Inghean pulled out of the sale. She paid off fees and let the townland talk about her dramatic failed dealings. In a supermarket a woman told Inghean she'd always thought she was a bit touched.

All the way back to when you were a teenager, the woman said. The punk rock hair and your long dresses.

Inghean flew back to the monastic corners of her apartment and wept for the fluff and scuts of the house she had grown up in. Dog-hairs in the sugar bowl and wagtails dancing the Charleston on the window sill.

She told the man she had a long-term renovation project. She would replace and adapt in keeping with the modest vernacular elements. Maybe turn cut-stone barns into artists' studios. She said horses, too, and maybe a wolfhound.

Everyone has a face-lift project, he said. Everyone wants to bring mammy and daddy's house back to former glory. But you can never get rid of the oldness. People are knocking them to the ground these days and building something modern on the same spot.

He was back tapping on the tablet, and smiling in a small, weary way.

In any case, the rehabilitation of one's former home is not a sufficient and compelling reason. Did you say wolfhound? Are you wise? The size. All the illnesses.

She was sickeningly thirsty from the gravel dust blowing round the shelter.

My brother's house was in a magazine, she told the man. He's coming to collect me when I'm finished here.

Nobody gets collected, the man said. They get dismissed and get on the next bus, or they don't.

The woman was back and standing before them.

I'm tempted to ask you if that's what I think it is, she said, pointing at the fascination on the Perspex, but I won't. Because if it's not you'll think I'm the world's worst!

It was hard to tell if she was addressing Inghean or the man. The man glanced up in vexation. How long had they been working together? This might be their first week or they'd been shaking people down for years in small offices.

I don't believe her, the woman said. She swung round to Inghean.

I don't believe you, she said. There isn't an old house and there isn't a project. The records will easily show. I'm going into the records.

Tapping, clicking, crunching on the gravel.

So there is an old house. Correction, there was an old house. No, wait. My mistake. There is an old house. And you nearly sold it.

The man looked on with that same smile, this time a little sadder. His eyes followed the sound of the horse.

I'll book her onto blue, he said. They'll take it from there.

Inghean's foot was in a bad cramp and if she stood up she would topple.

We can't have prevarication, the woman said, her voice soft again for the first time since they'd sat together on the bench and talked of the single life. Not when competition is so fierce. I'm sure you understand.

The man clipped his tablet closed after one last click and swipe.

It's a matter of commitment, he said. You didn't sell the old place. You didn't knock it to the ground to rebuild. We've seen this before. Testing the waters. I've an assistant back at the field office who calls it butterflying.

She did have plans. They had taken longer to come to fruition, that was all. She had laid them down like sediment over years and now, because of all that time, they were rock-solid. She wondered which of them would fly in her face first.

Millions and millions, he said. Is that what you're saying? There's a new word for millions of years. Did you know that? Ma, the archaeologists say.

He bleated like a lamb.

Ma. Three hundred and fifty ma!

The woman tapped Inghean's hand lightly.

This isn't the end, she said. You should know that. Blue isn't the end of the line. You'll have time during the next stage to build a case. I've seen it happen. I've known one or two who rose to the occasion.

The man was worried about the sound of the horse. There was something not right about it.

I saw a horse go down making sounds like that one time. Fresh grass, that spring stuff that's so green it doesn't look real. Killed it in the stomach.

Inghean wouldn't know where to start with raising horses. When she and her brother were children they had pointed at an old woman called Miss Maunsell. She'd lost her arm decades before, nobody knew how, and she went about with a tucked and pinned sleeve. Horses, it was said, a hunting accident. All the children regarded her with horror, as they would a frightful artefact from a brutal time and place.

Even a wolfhound would be too demanding and die too soon. She should ask her brother. He had been genial to the cats of the recluses next door. She once suggested he adopt something, maybe several. He said she was way off the mark, he didn't have time to share with animals. He said the whole country had gone mad for pets and their products and toys. It reminded him of America.

The woman and the man stood conferring about what was etched up there in the top corner. Their voices were low and intimate. One of them stifled a laugh, one of them raised a tablet to photograph the mystery. A cloud of terns swam overhead and scudded past fields and townlands. Coming from somewhere to go somewhere else, they stopped only to refuel in the estuaries. Everyone knew that and accepted the loss.

The Rakes of Mallow

We never have dreams in which we star for good or bad. We bronze where we used to burn. We arrive the hour after happy hour. We watch for dark centres in freckles. We pack into photos. We continue past the midnight hour. We've heard that that's when love comes tumbling down. We've been told that women ought to lean in. We retake photos until all parties approve. We elbow our spots at the table. We scroll until we *Like*. We recuse ourselves from remarks on the climate. We give thumbs up. We prove susceptible to conspiracies. We've been told we're the bigger part of the problem. We are afraid to cook heretofore unknown fish. We ate salmon when we were told it was all about omega 3s. We overfished the world's waters. We pluck translucent catfish hairs from the sides of our mouths. We retouch photos for the up-glow. We are at one at night with our reading apps. We don't have the full version yet of how we got here. We favour thrillers without missing or dismembered women and television series that don't expect us to solve a true crime. We donate money to send Plan B to girls in cruel, unusual regions. We believe whoever it was that said, *no second acts in American lives, except in the case of New York*. We never believed in New York. We turn the wheel to 270 degrees like our fathers in their small second-hand cars. We have taken down neighbours' fine fences in our time. We hydroplane safely when needs must. We never brake into the skid.

We scraped and washed plates in the kitchens of the cities where we first made landfall. We wore aprons too big a rigging for our bones. We graduated to chopped vegetables. We got stuck on carrots as our specialty. We let our fingers go chronic orange like smokers. We never smoked in those alleys. We lined up carrots, onions, celery. We were careful with the genial tricolours. We cascaded them into ripping hot pans and pots as big as babies' baths. We patted the shoulders of bussers and moppers whose countries were bombed to a blot. We went home with weary fry oil in our hair. We graduated to the raw bars. We repelled cold hands in the no-man's-land of loading docks. We informed customers about the shellfish of New England like experts who'd grown up basking in those waters. We studied chefs' words like *address* and *approach* when it came to the raw materials. We brushed off threats of being locked in the meat locker. We took home what would go uneaten. We learned the names and birthdays of wines from the upper echelon. We addressed clams called cherry stones and tiny necks. We approached their cute parochial names. We brought sent-back tuna steaks to the subway revenants. We wore the chainmail glove. We turned and tore our blades around oysters. We made ragged scrapes until creatures from three bodies of water lay open. We believed them vulnerable as tongues. We sent their shells to middens that were sent to stabilise concrete for bridges. We refused to drop majestic black lobsters into hissing pots. We didn't believe the humane trick with the knife behind the eyes.

We minded the children of financial advisors and entrepreneurs in pretty brick streets. We swung them high and sent them screaming down slides. We held their waists as they went hand by hand across bars. We sat on old benches where men with longing, red-edged eyes stopped to say hello. We met on corners with blue signs nicknamed after famous and dead neighbourhood people. We watched ghost bikes slide down fences and lose their flowers. We told each other where to get free dentistry done by students. We recalled their knees on our chests in root canal extremis. We invoked possible loss of sensation forever despite the duty of care. We scooped up fallen children. We blotted their knees and palms. We avoided all talk of tax time. We believed April to be the cruellest month. We watched parents trickle in from work that didn't look like work on their faces. We relinquished our charges. We felt their small hands hold us to stay and play for longer. We went back to small apartments under hot eaves and down in the cool bowels of brownstones. We slept on futons beside box fans turned up to five. We told the red wet brick streets we loved them because we had chosen them. We couldn't sleep without two pillows. We passed bay windows brightly inviting as grottos. We drank coffee behind the cordon. We observed the prices of flights climb the air. We mooched grass malls down the middle of boulevards. We never caught the price drop. We learned the names of baroque desserts from the doors of restaurants. We watched tartufo brought to table as devotionally as bombs. We saw children crack the shell. We packed little bags for nights on the Capes but never the islands. We made the sand squeak underfoot on the one beach known for a longing sound. We let the little triumphs accumulate unknown.

We peregrinated to suburbs to tend the children of professors and technocrats. We took early trains from leaking stations to pretty college towns. We joined their doty libraries and brought our parcels to their historically columned post offices. We got picked up in snow and rain. We walked uphill in spring. We fed wrathful toddlers in the lonely eminence of their highchairs. We met teenagers dripping in heartbreak home from school. We did the tampon run. We broke cups and plates that came down the generations. We glued stuff scrupulously like people with dinosaurs in the great halls of museums. We washed the muck from cleats. We learned about preservation societies. We had our favourite Latter Day Saints. We did the ice-cream run. We figured out the price per foot. We read massive books on the history of empire. We only knew our stuff about the British. We were ashamed of our lack of depth and range. We watched bickering and smacking on the studio floor television. We discerned how many people died intestate and left their spoiled offspring at war. We copied plant-based recipes from big books kept on high shelves. We loitered in kitchens where professors wanted to download their days. We learned that the humanities were dying along with more important species on the planet. We spoke our own language as a taste we didn't trust in our mouths. We accepted invitations to parties in local parks. We snubbed Hallowe'en-themed doughnuts and smash cakes. We never brought plus-ones. We warded off advances in utility rooms and SUVs. We said our visas were in eternal good standing. We helped with the clean-up. We got photos of graduations. We got teary about the toddlers who later looked like supermodels and all the messy years between. We got dropped at train stations in the clingy darkness.

We trained up and worked front of house. We infiltrated offices like spies on impossible missions. We temped at desks evacuated by leaves of absence and quiet little quittings. We re-trained in night classes. We dropped in on wires and evaded the sensors. We worked payroll and talent acquisition. We learned most things on the job. We talked a good game and talked up a storm and talked in the positive, eternal present. We displayed warmth and approachability when it came to questions about our origins. We took promotion as our due. We stayed on top of when we were up for the next one. We learned to move to force an issue. We accepted glass plaques with our names and years in foggy writing. We refused the word *service* for what was just work. We turned silver bowls over in hopes of a meaningful line from a poem. We learned not to talk too long about promotion to the people we had forfeited. We sent them the price of extractor fans and tiles. We shared our good fortune. We knew ourselves for dereliction of duties. We tried to regain ground. We studied up on their health. We ceded ground when asked about our own wellbeing. We drank midweek at the midpoint price and gave ourselves bubbles on weekends. We delayed our routine screenings to two cycles of the Gregorian calendar and longer. We urged more soluble fibre upon them and less meat. We showed them dogs we gave homes to and cats we fed from the street. We assured them we lived second floor instead of basement. We deleted reminder notes about our black blood, our tremors, our swollen. We heard inspirational stories of hundred-year-old neighbours we had harassed as children. We learned about the Centenarian Bounty and the two-thousand plus euro for those who made that bracket. We renewed our vows not to become citizens. We assured them we'd choke on the question of guns.

We flew to funerals in midwinter when the days ate their tails down to tight balls of light. We took designated seats and stood in stygian low-ceilinged rooms. We flew in summer when heatwaves brought mourners out in short sleeves and plimsolls. We shook the hands of strangers with ancestrally familiar faces. We bought them the pricey whiskey. We fielded questions of why not great modern places like Auckland and Dubai. We showered money on nieces and nephews. We gauged whether they'd take us in if the worst came to the worst. We pledged not to be shawled babblers in their corners. We reminisced about changing their nappies and dabbing their backsides with rash cream. We knew they didn't remember our hands and the torrential diarrhoea we stemmed and sluiced away. We speculated on old saints' names for our elusive children. We thought Brigid and Columba. We factored in Fursey. We lamented Maxentia of Beauvais for her persecution and barbaric virgin death. We contemplated religious life but never found an order that would have us as members. We found second little homes by Gulf Shores and Finger Lakes. We watched men free lovers' sandals from tar like tending birds after the oil spill. We saw women wipe lovers' holiday foreheads with corners of neutral linen garments. We heard children cry in anguish at the last beloved ice cream on the last day at the beach. We danced with strangers in the subtropics. We dropped our hips around the kinky strangeness of four-four time. We listened to the last moments of the Mars Rover consumed in a dust storm. We accumulated the offbeat for friends who might witness our extinction. We built up reserves and caught falling knives and readied ourselves for middling odds. We forswore living in a country where winter solstice was prime-time news. We'd never win a ticket to join beetles and ghosts in the limelight of an ancient waiting room.

ACKNOWLEDGEMENTS

My thanks and appreciation go to:

Faith O'Grady, ever truer to her name and someone who urges books into life.

Declan Meade, a legend in his longtime dedication to the short form.

Editors at the journals and magazines where these stories reached their final form: *The Kenyon Review, The Common, The Dublin Review, SUBTROPICS, The Stinging Fly.*

Boston friends: fiction writers, poets, translators… you know who you are.

Liberal arts colleagues at Babson College, as well as the Peter M. Black Research Scholar fund that supported the work of many of these stories.

Editorial colleagues at *AGNI*, and all *AGNI* writers who have entrusted their work to me.

The Centre for Irish Studies and the Charles A. Heimbold Chair of Irish Studies programme; the English Department and ENG3680 students; and especially Dr. Jennifer Joyce at Villanova University: I completed this book in your gracious and encouraging atmosphere

My father, mother, and trio of sisters: the best of the west of Ireland.

My husband, James McNaughton, and stepdaughter, Niamh McNaughton, in their highly original talent for life.

And the vivid memory of Monica Higgins (Boston) and Keyser Wilson (Tuscaloosa), rake and dandy both.